W9-DJG-345

"I have to keep my daughters' best interests in mind, and I've seen some things that disturb me."

Sharon fiddled with her doughnut, dunking it but not eating it. "They've become attached to you, in such a short time. That worries me, because I think. . ." Her dunks became more frequent, her doughnut smaller as sodden chunks fell away; still she didn't meet his gaze. "I think they expect more to come from this association than will happen. And I don't want them hurt." Her eyes lifted to his. "You understand my position, don't you?"

"I'm trying to." Jared watched her closely. "So you think we should talk to them? Explain things?" He had numerous nieces and nephews but didn't really know the first thing when it came to dealing with children.

"Actually. . ." She looked down at her coffee again. "I think it would be better if we just stop this before they get hurt."

"Stop this?" Jared didn't look away from her. "You mean stop seeing each other?"

"You make it sound like a whole lot more than it is," Sharon accused, and Jared looked down, acknowledging the truth of what she'd said. "This was supposed to be all about friendship, Jared. Nothing more."

"You're right. I'm sorry. That came out wrong."

God had told him one thing; Sharon told him another. Free will had everything to do with a person's future. He couldn't force Sharon to change her mind; he wasn't that type of person.

"So since we hardly know each other," she continued, "and since upon knowing each other, things haven't always worked out well. . ." Her words trailed off, and he knew she meant Andy. "I think it best if we just keep our distance from now on."

PAMELA GRIFFIN lives in Texas and divides her time between family, church activities, and writing. She fully gave her life to the Lord in 1988 after a rebellious young adulthood and owes the fact that she's still alive today to an all-loving and forgiving God and a mother who prayed that her wayward daughter would come "home." Pamela's main goal in writing Christian romance is to encourage others through entertaining stories that also heal the wounded spirit.

Please visit Pamela at: www.Pamela-Griffin.com.

Books by Pamela Griffin

HEARTSONG PRESENTS

Don't miss out on any of our super romances. Write to us at the following address for information on our newest releases and club information.

Heartsong Presents Readers' Service
PO Box 721
Uhrichsville, OH 44683

Or visit www.heartsongpresents.com

Sweet, Sugared Love

Pamela Griffin

Heartsong Presents

Much thanks to Therese Travis, Theo Igrisan, and my mother for all their help. For my sons—thank you for your suggestions, Brandon, and to Joshua for his idea of a prank. To my Lord, who may not always give us what we think we want—but never fails to keep His promises concerning a better future and the dreams He has for us.

A note from the Author:
I love to hear from my readers! You may correspond with me by writing:

Pamela Griffin
Author Relations
PO Box 721
Uhrichsville, OH 44683

ISBN 978-1-59789-619-1

SWEET, SUGARED LOVE

Copyright © 2007 by Pamela Griffin. All rights reserved. Except for use in any review, the reproduction or utilization of this work in whole or in part in any form by any electronic, mechanical, or other means, now known or hereafter invented, is forbidden without the permission of Heartsong Presents, an imprint of Barbour Publishing, Inc., PO Box 721, Uhrichsville, Ohio 44683.

All scripture quotations are taken from the King James Version of the Bible.

All of the characters and events in this book are fictitious. Any resemblance to actual persons, living or dead, or to actual events is purely coincidental.

Our mission is to publish and distribute inspirational products offering exceptional value and biblical encouragement to the masses.

PRINTED IN THE U.S.A.

one

"Maybe if you pray hard enough, Jared, God will drop your future wife on your doorstep."

As he drove his horse-drawn wagon along the one-lane dirt road rimmed with white pines, Jared Crisp shook his head at the memory of his brother Brandon's teasing words.

On a day like this, he'd decided against taking the car. The invigorating air felt good against his face as he made his bimonthly deliveries of his family's maple syrup. Besides, tourists got such a kick out of his old-fashioned mode of transportation, especially the children.

On these late spring mornings, the local kids often gathered on sidewalks or played games in their front yards. The *clip-clop* of Tamany's hooves along the asphalt of the main road drew them forward, flocking to him as if he were the ice-cream man. He patted his pocket to assure himself he'd remembered the treats to dole out to small, eager hands, then withdrew one for himself and unwrapped it, popping a maple candy disc into his mouth.

Buttery and sugary, the candy melted on his tongue, the sweet creamy flavor a time-honored blend his great-grandfather had dreamed up when he first started making and canning maple syrup. Perhaps his family was a bit on the old-fashioned side, and some of the teenage boys did look at him with raised brows as they drove past in their sports cars, but there was steadfastness in family tradition that the entire Crisp family upheld with staunch regard.

And that included Jared finding himself a wife.

He had begun to wonder if God forgot His promise to him

years ago. His three married brothers—all younger—taunted him mercilessly about his desire to hold out until God brought Jared the woman He had chosen especially for him. In high school, he'd dated, nothing serious or steady. A tragedy in his senior year involved a troubled classmate committing suicide over another friend of Jared's had brought him closer to His Savior. And one day during deep prayer, he felt as if God told him not to seek a wife, but that He would bring the woman Jared was to marry to Goosebury. Some of the women who'd grown up with Jared had shown interest—Jared wasn't blind—but he saw no sense in dating if it could never lead to anything serious. Why get mired in a relationship that involved deep emotions and could only inflict pain when it ended? When Jared met his future wife, he would know; the Lord had shown him that. And he wanted his heart to be whole, not scarred from past love interests.

Let his brothers scoff; Jared didn't care. He knew the wait, though at times trying, would be well worth the effort when the day came. Yet he didn't want to be as old as Abraham when that glorious day arrived.

"I'll be hitting thirty-three come December," he said under his breath. "But you already know that, God. So any time you're ready to set me up with a life mate will be fine with me."

A shout from up ahead made Jared crack a smile as the first of his young friends spotted him. He brought the wagon to a halt and soon bright, smiling faces and eager pleas surrounded him. When he'd filled all eight of the outstretched hands, the children talked with him, a few petting Tamany, who bore their sticky hands and awkward pats like a real trooper, flicking her ears and giving a little toss of her head now and then as if in agreement with the conversation. Jared sensed the old bay loved the attention.

"My mom had to take me to the dentist the last time you

come," said Jimmy, [...]
captured the town's heart[...]
Dennis the Menace. Jared ha[...]
labeling the boy "Jim-Jim the Peri[...]

"I chipped a tooth. See?" Jimmy o[...]
pointed to an incisor. "The doc had to fil[...]
look sharper?" he asked with the hopeful tone o[...]
pleasure in pointing out his physical battle scars, m[...]
pirate with a peg leg and eye patch.

"It sure does," Jared agreed, at which the boy's face beame[...]
"But better be more careful in the future, Jimmy. Those candies were made to be sucked on and enjoyed, not bit into so they end up breaking all your teeth."

"Oh, it's okay. Mom said she needed a good excuse to get me to the dentist anyway."

Jared shook his head in amusement. He had a feeling Jimmy's munching days wouldn't end. He said good-bye to the children and continued on to his aunts' souvenir store. The citizens of Goosebury dearly respected and loved both of his father's elderly sisters, even if they were somewhat senile and had a habit of finishing one another's sentences, at times creating confusion.

He pulled the horse and wagon up before the small log A'bric & A'brac store, which also fronted their home. Once he tied Tamany to the post, Jared easily hefted the last carton of Crisp's Maple Syrup from the back of the wagon. He often made his aunts' store his last stop, since they always invited him to the noon meal, and Jared never declined their great cooking.

As he opened the door, the silver chimes tinkled a greeting to all within. He saw no sign of his aunts. Behind the counter, a woman faced the wall of shelves, her back to Jared. Light blond hair escaped out of some contraption holding her hair up high and letting it hang down in thick, messy waves that appealed. Jeans and a pink T-shirt clad her trim figure. Of gh his heart.

ump as reali-

other curbing

with alarm. He

, but she backed up

"Um,   t back."

Without awaiting   to the curtain shield-
ing the dining room as fast   d be considered normal.
Sharon had recently moved to Goosebury at her friend Leslie's
urging, thinking the town peaceful and safe. She had temporarily
stayed at her friend's renovated barn near Leslie and her husband,
Blaine's, home until half a month earlier when she found her
present job and rented Loretta Crisp Mallory's larger house. This
month had been the first time she'd relaxed in years.

Now she wasn't so sure that this town didn't have its own
brand of crackpots.

Catching sight of plump and gentle Loretta, she hurried
toward her. Tall and bubbly, Josephine Crisp, Loretta's sister,
stood nearby as they both inventoried a delivery of mementos.
Sharon had learned during her first day in their employment
that Loretta was a wartime widow who'd moved into their
parents' old home with Josephine, a spinster. They had con-
verted the huge front parlor into a small souvenir shop that
also specialized in antiques. The only one in town like it—the
only one Sharon had ever heard of—the hominess of the
atmosphere gave an old-fashioned, mid-twentieth-century

flair to the place. Open at ten o'clock, A'bric & A'brac closed its doors at five sharp, when the sisters retreated to the back of the house to carry on with their daily lives.

"Whatever is the matter, dear?" Josephine asked. "You look like—"

"You saw a ghost," Loretta finished for her.

"There's some weirdo out there," Sharon explained. "A real crackpot. He said something, well pretty suggestive...in a way. It sort of rattled me."

"Oh, dear." Loretta set down the miniature of a ceramic covered bridge. "We can't have that. It must be a tourist. Everyone in Goosebury is reasonably sane. Perhaps—"

"We should investigate," Josephine concluded.

"Yes, please. I hope you don't mind."

"Nonsense," Josephine said with a smile, putting her arm around Sharon.

"We take care of our own," Loretta confirmed.

The two women bustled toward the shop. Unable to quench her curiosity, Sharon followed and peered through the curtain.

To her astonishment, Loretta hugged the candidate for the asylum. "Jared! It's so good to see you. I'm delighted you're feeling better. It's always lovely to see Thomas, but—"

"We missed you," Josephine finished with a welcoming smile. "Colds can be such nasty things. I do hope you enjoyed the spiced cider we sent with Thomas?"

"It was great. Even if it was out of season."

"Oh, pish," Josephine scoffed. "Just because it's a Christmas tradition doesn't mean it can't—"

"Help heal one's bones all year round," Loretta finished with a smile.

The man they called Jared looked over Loretta's shoulder and spotted Sharon peeking through the drape. Before she could retreat, the sisters turned to look.

"Sharon, dear, the crackpot must have left. Jared here is the only one in the store—"

"So all's safe now."

Sharon felt the burn of her face and wondered if it had achieved the glow of maroon. She saw the corners of the man's mouth twitch. Aggravation that he found the situation amusing made her square her shoulders and step forward.

"Come here, dear. We'd like you to meet—"

"Our nephew Jared Crisp. His father—our brother—is head of Crisp Maple Syrup. It's a family owned business. Have we told you? Our great-grandfather by many generations—"

"Started making maple syrup years ago, but all the family has a part in it, however small."

"Jared, meet Sharon Lester," Loretta said, oblivious to the tension between the two. Jared and Sharon continued to observe one another—Jared working hard to contain his amusement, Sharon with narrowed eyes. "She moved to Goosebury, what was it—two months ago?"

"Almost." Sharon was surprised at how calm her voice sounded. "A month and a half."

"So, you just moved here. . . ." A wondering note touched his words, the reason for which Sharon didn't care to speculate. She eyed his offered hand as suspect, but with the two sisters watching, she had little choice but to receive his greeting.

His hand felt warm, strong; his fingers long, encasing her much smaller hand. Uneasy, she withdrew hers before he could fully shake it.

So this was the nephew about whom she'd heard nothing but glowing reports during the evenings she and the children shared his aunts' table. Curious, she took inventory since he seemed unable to take his eyes off her face. His hair, dark and thick, grew a little long to his collar. His face was strong, lean; his nose straight and long; and his eyes. . .

She felt her heart give a strange flutter as she met his eyes, which had not stopped gazing into hers. She hadn't noticed his eyes before. A mixture of gray, pale green, even silver combined with black lashes and dark brows, his eyes were striking.

Disconcerted, she averted her gaze to Loretta—another mistake, because the woman beamed at her as if she possessed a secret. Josephine's expression matched her sister's. The two had done nothing but extol the virtues of their extraordinary nephew to Sharon for weeks, and she sensed matchmaking imminent in their plans. Jared was out of the ordinary, all right—and granted, he could turn a number of heads—but he was also clearly insane. Besides, she never planned to marry again.

She was saved by the bell—literally—as the door swung open and two of her children stampeded inside, breathless.

"Mama! Mama!"

With satisfaction, Sharon noted Jared's startled expression of disappointment. Maybe she didn't have to worry about his pursuit of her after all.

"Kitty—Mindy—walk, don't run. Where's Andy?" Sharon looked beyond them for sight of her twelve-year-old son.

"He's with the moose," six-year-old Kitty exclaimed, her eyes bright with excitement.

"The *moose*?"

"The mama moose got hit by a car or something," her ten-year-old explained. "And left a baby moose behind. Andy's with it."

"Oh, dear," Loretta said. "Wild moose—"

"Can be dangerous," Josephine finished.

Alarm chilled Sharon's blood. "Where is he?"

"Near the crossroads by the interstate," Mindy said.

"The interstate." Sharon struggled not to let her fear show. "I told you children not to leave the main square."

"My wagon's out front," Jared said, his tone concerned,

sober, "if you need a ride."

Sharon owned no car; neither did Loretta or Josephine—not one in working order anyway. Still, she hesitated. Walking had never presented a problem; most everything needed stood within close range of the shop. Yet she must get to Andy quickly. Since Jared was the sisters' nephew, Sharon hoped that made her acceptance of his offer of a ride safe and that he wouldn't resort to any hidden psychopathic tendencies.

She gave him a slight nod and turned to her oldest daughter. "Mindy, you come with me. Kitty, stay here."

"Mama!"

"Do as you're told."

"We have milk and cookies," Loretta coaxed.

"Would you like some?" Josephine added.

A somewhat pacified Kitty nodded, allowing Josephine to herd her to the back and the kitchen.

Sharon remembered she was supposed to be on the clock. "You don't mind me leaving?"

"Of course not. You go with Jared and get your son."

Loretta's sympathetic eyes comforted Sharon, and again she felt the peculiar warmth to know someone cared for her.

Outside, her abrupt pace halted when she saw the horse and wagon. "You mean this? I thought you meant a station wagon."

"Tamany can get us there fast," Jared assured. "I know a short-cut. Most cars can't travel it because it's a dirt road and uneven.

"Neat!" Mindy exclaimed, needing no persuasion to jump into the back of the old-fashioned vehicle.

Sharon said nothing, ignoring his helping hand as she climbed onto the seat. She reminded herself that this man was the sisters' nephew and that they knew of her location and that she was in his company. Really, though, it shouldn't come as a surprise that someone with a few screws absent in his noggin would be driving a horse and buggy in the twenty-first century.

two

Jared drove Tamany to the area Mindy directed him, extremely conscious of the silent woman sitting on the other end of the wagon seat. Accustomed to the ribbing he received from his brothers and having learned to laugh at himself and take things in stride, he hadn't let his aunts' mix-up regarding the identity of Sharon's "crackpot" embarrass him too much. He'd found the whole thing rather amusing, though Sharon obviously did not.

Frustrated, he crunched down hard on the sliver of his candy disc. He would have offered Mindy a piece, but her mother would probably insist on inspecting it first to make sure he hadn't laced it with cyanide.

How could he have been so stupid to say what he had to her? Granted, the surety that swept through him had floored him, but such a first impression hadn't won him favor. Still, seeing two of her three kids bound through the door convinced Jared he must have gotten some wires crossed and been mistaken at the connection. He still could hardly believe the children were hers; she looked as if she were a college girl in her early twenties, not a mom with a brood of kids.

Knowing this was no time for small talk, he curbed his desire to learn more about this family and struggled to keep his questions inside. Where was Sharon's husband? His aunts had seemed pleased to introduce Jared to her, or had he misread their actions, as well?

Near the turnoff to the interstate, Jared spotted a dark-haired boy off the side of the road. He stood a few feet away but alarmingly close to a pale, dusty-brown moose calf.

13

"Andy," Sharon called out at the top of her voice as the boy turned upon their approach. "Get away from that animal!"

At the clopping of Tamany's hooves, the moose calf turned its ungainly head to look. To Jared's surprise, it remained still, and he wondered if seeing the horse, another creature on four legs, had helped to ease any panic the animal must feel; had he driven a noisy car, the moose would have fled, Jared was sure. That it stood on tall, skinny legs near the boy and had not run away amazed him. He imagined the little fellow felt lost without its mother and uncertain of what to do.

"Mom!" the boy cried out as Jared brought Tamany to a halt and Sharon jumped down. "Look what I found. Can I keep her?"

A girl moose, Jared mentally corrected.

"Of course not." Sharon approached boy and moose with caution. Jared also left the wagon, unsure. The calf was young, no more than a couple of weeks old he would guess, but it was still wild. At this stage of life, the calf resembled a baby deer, stockier in build, and stood as tall as the boy's waist. If it panicked, it might get hurt.

"But she's got no one else. Her mama got hit by a car or something." He pointed. "Over there."

Jared looked in the direction Andy pointed. In the distance, a massive carcass lay at the side of the road.

"And just why you're out this far from the shop is what I want to know," Sharon said, her voice grim.

The boy quirked his lips to the side but didn't reply.

"Why did the mama go into the road?" Mindy asked curious.

"Probably to lick the salt from it, if there's any left this late in the season," Jared responded. "They need it for their diet."

"There's salt in the road?" The girl's eyes grew round. "Why would anyone salt the road? It's not like people are going to eat it or anything."

"Mom, please," Andy begged. "We could put her in that old

barn at the back of the house. We can't just leave her here for a grizzly bear or a wolf or some other killer animal to find. We just can't!"

"The boy has a point," Jared said, earning him a sharp glare from Sharon. "The calf is still nursing. Most calves stay with their mothers through the first year of their lives and aren't able to fend for themselves or understand all the dangers of predators."

"And just how do you know so much about moose calves, Mr. Crisp?" she asked, her words quiet but no less barbed.

"My sister-in-law works with the wildlife reserve."

His steady answer curbed a further reply, and he watched as her mouth formed a silent "oh."

"I have some rope in the back of the wagon. We can lead the calf to your barn, and I'll call Becca, my sister-in-law, to inform her of the situation."

"Please, Mom," the boy pleaded again. Within his narrowed eyes, a darker blue than Sharon's, Jared sensed both desperation and the prelude to angry resentment should she refuse.

"Oh, all right," she said at last. "But only until someone from the wildlife department can come and cart it away."

"Do you have a cell phone?" he asked Sharon. "I can call Becca right now."

"I'm sorry. I don't."

With no means to contact his sister-in-law, Jared saw no alternative but to try to lasso a moose.

As he retrieved the rope and the small family stood on the sidelines to watch, he knew he looked foolish and felt more than a little ridiculous. Sharon must already think him a dolt, but he wondered what Becca would say to his plan. He hoped he wasn't breaking any laws connected to wildlife. He knew leaving the young untouched was vital to their well-being, but in the case of an orphan, he felt there must be extenuating circumstances.

Knowing that moose had poor eyesight, which could work in his favor, he asked Andy to talk to the calf in quiet tones and approached it from behind. Its long ears flicked back, as if it heard him, and Jared sensed that coming up and suddenly slipping the lasso around its neck might scare it worse and cause it to bolt.

He considered what he was about to do, knowing it would forever mark him as a lunatic in Sharon's mind, with no hope of rectifying his earlier mistake—but it was the only solution he could think of at the moment.

"'Amazing grace! How sweet the sound,'" he sang in a gentle tenor, hoping not only that it would help calm the calf and alert the animal to his presence but also work as a silent prayer heavenward for help. "'That saved a wretch like me. . .'"

He moved closer; the moose remained still.

"'I once was lost, but now am found; was blind, but now I see.'" As he sang the last line, he gently dropped the large noose over the compact head and long snout. The animal lumbered a step forward in shock, but Jared tightened the rope, keeping a firm grip on it. He stood very still and sang another verse to quiet the calf, even reaching up to lay his hand on its bristly hide in reassurance. It must have been too young to consider humans a threat.

Mission accomplished. Now Jared wondered how he would lead the animal to the wagon.

"Andy, grab some twigs with fresh green leaves and bring them here please." He hoped Sharon wouldn't mind his ordering around her son. The youth gave him a narrow-eyed glance but moved to do as he asked. "Walk slowly, so as not to scare it," he said when the moose gave a nervous jerk once the boy turned.

"What do you want with twigs?" Mindy wanted to know.

"Moose are herbivores. Do you know what that means?"

She shook her head, and he continued. "They eat plants. From what Becca told me, moose start eating solids early, and they have some of their teeth, so I think this might work."

Andy returned holding a handful of twigs.

"Great, now hold it out to the moose and slowly walk toward the wagon."

"I don't think so." Sharon stepped forward. "If that animal has teeth, it may bite. Didn't Loretta say wild moose are dangerous?"

"Mom, the twig is really long. I'll be careful."

Jared understood the boy wanting to take part in what he must consider a big adventure, but he also understood Sharon's fears. Rather than interfere, he let them work it out. Andy convinced his mom, while Jared stood, with as much patience as he could muster, hoping the calf wouldn't become nervous and bolt.

"First let it have a taste," Jared instructed, "but no more."

Andy held the tip of the long twig under the moose's nose, a leaf brushing its nostril. The animal sniffed the branch, its huge upper lip opening to nibble the tender leaves.

"Start walking backward," Jared instructed.

Andy did so, and the moose also moved, craning its neck for another bite. The boy kept the leaves just out of reach, and the moose continued to follow him with Jared keeping a loose rein on the rope.

Once at the back of the wagon, he tied the moose's rope to it and they took their places inside, Jared with a silent prayer of thanks. Both Andy and Mindy sat in back, to "watch" the calf as if afraid it might dissolve into thin air should they look away for a moment.

Jared picked up the reins and clicked his tongue for Tamany to walk. He kept up a slow and steady pace that the moose calf could follow. Mindy soon grew tired of watching and positioned herself between Sharon and Jared, leaning over the back of the seat.

"How come you sang to the moose?" she wanted to know.

"That must have seemed crazy," Jared admitted with a smile. He noticed Sharon didn't deny it. "When my grandfather was alive, he had an ornery horse that always quieted when he sang or hummed church hymns. I remembered him doing that when I was a boy, so I decided to try it, too."

"Why church hymns? Do other songs work?"

Jared shrugged. "Don't really know. Never tried before, and that's all my grandfather sang back then. He was in the church choir."

"Are you in the choir, too?"

"Well. . .yes." His face and ears grew warm at her personal questions.

"I didn't see you when we went last week."

"Mindy, that's enough," Sharon said quietly. "Maybe Mr. Crisp doesn't go to our church."

"Do you?" Mindy asked.

"I go to the same church that my aunts go to—Grace Fellowship—but I was out of town last week, and I was sick before that."

"That's the same one we go to!" the girl exclaimed, eager. "Me, Mama, Andy, and Kitty."

He noticed the omission of her father. "Your dad doesn't go there?" he asked.

He felt more than heard the seconds of significant silence. "Daddy died last year."

"Oh." Stunned, Jared refrained from looking Sharon's way. "I'm sorry."

"Do you know anything else besides church songs?" Mindy asked in a bright voice, as if unfazed by her admission of her father's death.

"I, uh. . .sure."

"Do you know 'Row, Row, Row Your Boat'?"

"Yup."

"Will you sing it with me? I'll start, and you follow."

Jared grinned. "Well now, it seems to me that song doesn't really fit our situation. How about we revise it a bit? Drive, drive, drive your wagon along the winding road. Horse and harness, moose and rope, a sight to behold."

He heard Sharon chuckle at his silly parody of the popular melody.

"Okay!" Mindy giggled. "But you start."

One following the other, they sang countless rounds of the song, though he noticed neither Sharon nor Andy joined in. When Jared neared the road intersecting with the town's main square, he stopped the wagon. "You'll have to tell me where you live," he explained to Sharon.

"We're renting Loretta's old house."

He nodded and headed about a mile down the lane that ran behind the shop to the yellow-shingled home nestled in the wood.

"How come we haven't seen you in town before?" Mindy wanted to know.

"This is a busy time of year on my family's farm."

"What do you do there?"

"Oh, plenty of things." He pulled the wagon into the drive in front of the barn and tied off the reins. "I'll tell you about it some time. Right now we should take care of the moose."

To Jared's relief, getting the animal into the empty barn didn't present a problem. The calf followed Jared as he led it by the rope and tied it to a post inside.

"Do you have to tie her up?" Andy's sulky tone matched his mutinous expression.

"I do if you don't want the moose bolting any time the barn

door opens." His answer seemed to pacify the youth.

"I'll give you a ride back to the shop," he told Sharon, "and I'll call Becca from there."

"I want to stay here," Andy said.

"No." Sharon's reply to her son was abrupt. "I don't want you alone with that moose."

"Aw, Mom. She's not going to hurt me. I was alone with her a long time before you got there."

"Yes, and we'll talk about that later," she said, her tone promising discipline. "Now come along."

"I wanna stay." He crossed his arms, rebellion clear in his wide-legged stance.

"I'm not going to argue with you, Andy. You're coming with us."

"No."

Uncomfortable with the rising tension between mother and son, and feeling in part responsible since he had a hand in delivering the moose, Jared cleared his throat. "The calf will need to eat. Maybe Andy could gather some horsetails, water lilies, pondweed—any other woody plants from the pond over yonder."

Sharon whipped her irritated gaze to his; Andy's narrowed eyes simmered with instant resentment aimed at Jared.

"It was just a thought," he explained, realizing he'd over-stepped the mark again.

To his surprise, Sharon gave a slow nod of agreement to his plan. "All right, Andy. You can stay, but I don't want you going anywhere near that moose while I'm gone. Gather the food, as Mr. Crisp suggested, since I don't want the thing starving before help gets here, but that's all. I get off work in two hours. If a worker from the preserve hasn't arrived by the time I get home, we'll both go in the barn to feed it."

The boy didn't respond, but Sharon turned to the wagon as if she considered the matter closed and was confident he would obey her instructions. Noting the boy's sultry expression, Jared wasn't so sure.

࠵

That evening, everyone sat at the Loretta and Josephine's dining table, clasping hands and bowing heads as Josephine said grace. Sharon closed her eyes and for a moment relaxed, as her action blocked out the sight of the man sitting across from her.

It hadn't surprised her that Josephine asked Jared to stay to supper since he'd missed lunch because of the moose; the man *was* the sisters' nephew. And it didn't surprise her that the sisters increased their efforts to interest Sharon in Jared—and for the same reason. What did surprise her was that he seemed more uncomfortable than she felt. The realization that she was a widow with three children must have played a large factor in his unease.

Loretta and Josephine merrily ordered the supper conversation, playing off each other's sentences as always, seemingly unaware of the tension between their guests. As for the children, Mindy ate her food with silent, single-minded concentration, Kitty played with hers, and Andy wolfed his down like the place was about to blow up and he had to get out of there before it did. Sharon had only taken a few bites when Andy rocketed up and headed for the door.

"Andy!" she called after him. "Finish your supper."

"I am finished," he said without turning around. "I'm going outside."

Before Sharon could correct his manners or behavior, he disappeared from sight, and the door slammed, announcing his departure.

"I apologize," she said to the two sisters. "I have no idea what's gotten into him lately."

She squirmed at the half-truth. Andy hated his father and

what he'd done to them, but until several months ago when Sharon received the phone call from prison with the news of Mark's death, Andy had always nurtured his animosity with quiet deliberation. Since then, he had become sullen and rebellious.

"That's perfectly all right, dear," Loretta said. "Boys—"

"Will be boys," Josephine finished. "Why I remember Jared was quite the handful." She chuckled. "Such a prankster. You never knew—"

"When he'd hit next," Loretta ended. "There was that time in the root cellar with the flour—"

Jared choked on his iced lemonade. "Aunt Loretta, I doubt Sharon and her girls would be interested in hearing that story."

Sharon eyed his reddened face and decided to take pity on him. "If Mr. Crisp would rather we not know—"

"Well, I wanna know," Mindy jumped in. "What did he do, Mrs. Loretta?"

Loretta looked at Sharon, uncertain, then at Mindy. "I suppose that's something you'll have to ask him yourself, Mindy."

Mindy turned pleading eyes his way, and Jared let out a resigned breath. "I covered myself in flour and scared my cousin into thinking I was a ghost. She ran into the kitchen, banged into the table, and knocked over the jars of applesauce my mom was canning. Three crashed to the floor—none of them had lids on them yet."

Kitty giggled.

"Tell them the rest, Jared," Josephine urged, a twinkle in her eye.

"The rest. Yeah, right." His eyes, bearing a gleam of sheepish amusement, moved from Kitty to Sharon. "My mom turned around, saw me in the doorway, and took a step back in shock. When she did, she stepped on the cat's tail. It yowled and scratched her ankle. Mom dropped the pan of hot applesauce and bent over in pain to grab her ankle or the cat—no one knows which. The cat raced away and knocked over the broom. The handle hit mom in the head."

Sharon felt her mouth twitch.

"Go on, Jared. Finish it."

"There's more?" Mindy asked with a squeal of delight and the thrill of discovering another's humorous scrapes.

"Yeah, unfortunately there is." Jared smiled at Mindy. "My aunt—my mom's sister—came running into the room to see what all the commotion was about. She slipped and fell in the applesauce. When Susie—my cousin—ran screaming from the cellar where I'd scared her, she opened the front door and let the dog inside. It came bounding into the kitchen, saw the cat, and gave it a merry chase through the kitchen. The dog and cat slid and ran through the applesauce—then into the parlor and over Mom's newly covered chairs."

Sharon could no longer contain her mirth. She laughed, tears filling her eyes. Jarred grinned at her amusement.

"My dad came in, caught the dog, and hauled it outside, and that was the end of that."

"Did you get in trouble?" Mindy wanted to know through her giggles.

"Uh, yup. You could say that."

"Almost every day of the week," Josephine finished for him. "You might say our dear Jared was always in the thick of things."

He gave an embarrassed grin and shook his head.

The atmosphere had lightened considerably. Loretta wiped tears of mirth from her eyes with her napkin.

"Say," Josephine began. "Jared, you mentioned earlier that you had to go into the city this week, and, Sharon, you mentioned yesterday how you haven't been able to find any slim-size jeans in town to fit Andy or clothes for Kitty. Wednesday's your day off. I'm sure Jared wouldn't mind taking you into the city."

She beamed at Jared, who looked as trapped as Sharon felt.

"I wouldn't want to impose," Sharon said quickly.

"Nonsense. It would be no imposition, would it, Jared?" Loretta asked, aiding Josephine's cause.

His uncertain smile flickered. "No imposition at all." Sharon realized he said the only polite thing he could under the circumstances.

"Really, it isn't necessary." Sharon fidgeted with her napkin, wiping her mouth though it didn't need it.

"Well, dear, to be honest, I have no idea when the coupe will be fixed to run such a distance without stalling—"

"And you did mention all of Andy's jeans had holes in the knees," Loretta reminded.

Sharon withheld a sigh. Lately, her son whisked through a pair of jeans in less than a month, and the small children's-clothes shop contained a very scant selection of size 6X clothes for Kitty when she'd shopped there.

"I really don't mind." Jared's eyes were kind, his tone softer, more sincere as Sharon looked up at him.

"Neatness," Mindy said. "Will you drive the horse and wagon?"

"I hadn't planned on it." He looked at Sharon. "I *do* own a car. I take Tamany when I make my rounds because tourists get such a kick out of seeing an old-fashioned horse-drawn buggy."

Feeling pushed into a corner but not wanting to be rude or disappoint Jared's aunts since they'd done so much for her and her family, Sharon gave a slight nod. "All right. Thank you." She squeezed the words from a tight throat.

She still thought the man a lunatic, but he didn't appear dangerous. When he'd sung one of her favorite hymns to the moose calf, he'd floored Sharon. But when he explained his motive later, she'd understood his reasoning. His actions and the gentle way he'd handled the orphaned moose as well as his ability to laugh at himself and make others laugh with him made Sharon realize the man did possess some admirable traits.

But dating him was out of the question, and she would need to get that across to the two sisters as soon as possible once he left.

She had a feeling it would be easier to lasso a moose.

three

Sharon eyed the pleasant young woman who was inspecting the moose calf for possible injuries. She noted Becca's teasing affection for her brother-in-law, whom she treated as a beloved family member.

"I hope I didn't break any laws," Jared said in worry as he hunched down beside Becca.

"Hmm." Becca deliberated. "She's such a young one. A couple of weeks old at the most." She let out a sad little sigh, but her brown eyes danced with mischief as she glanced at Jared. "Feeding her wasn't the best of ideas, but I understand the situation, and I really do think it ingenious how you got her here. I wish I'd been a bird in a tree to see that. You singing to a moose." Becca laughed.

"At least I had a captive audience," Jared joked back.

"Yeah, well, with your voice, you always do. Believe me, if I hadn't been out of town, I would've come here straightaway. I'm sorry you had to keep the moose overnight."

"So are you saying we shouldn't have fed her?" Sharon asked. "Were the plants not good for her stomach since she's so young?"

Becca directed a look to the door, glimpsing where the children gathered around her truck. Andy had left the barn only at Sharon's insistence. She hadn't wanted him in the vicinity when they discussed the moose's fate.

"What you did won't hurt her," Becca assured. "Jared was right about that. But when a person feeds a moose, it can present a problem. The animal can grow to expect it from everyone, and later, when it's grown, it can attack a person if not offered food. Some moose have had to be killed because they presented that very danger."

"That's terrible," Sharon said. "Neither of us meant to do anything wrong; Andy was only trying to help." She didn't mention that when she'd found his bed unslept in that morning, she'd hurried to the barn to find Andy tucked in a sleeping bag a few feet away from the moose. Sharon's heart had almost stopped, though the scene she'd stumbled upon had been docile. Her son had slept while the moose calf opened its eyes at the squeak of the barn door and lifted its head. The calf had grown more alert, probably hoping for more of the leafy treats they'd fed her the previous evening.

Becca looked at Sharon with an understanding smile. "Andy did fine. This little girl will need a lot of care before we release her to the wild, if that's Hugh's decision. It depends on how she responds while in captivity."

"Then you've found someone who will take it?" Jared asked.

Becca nodded. "I talked with Hugh MacFarland last night on the phone, and he said to bring her in. He's a retired game warden who now works as a wildlife rehabilitator. His farm is ten miles from here."

"You're not taking my moose away, are you?"

No one had noticed the shadow that filled the barn door, blocking out the sunlight. Sharon sent a concerned glance to her son.

"Andy, we talked about this earlier—"

"I can take care of her," he interrupted, walking forward. "I can take real good care of her."

"I'm sure you can, Andy." Becca's tone was soft and sympathetic. "But wild moose don't make good pets."

"But she likes it here!" he insisted. "I want to keep her."

"A baby moose calf like this is fun to have around." Becca

agreed in understanding. "But they grow fast—and get bigger every day. In the animal kingdom, they're the fastest to grow."

"The barn is big," he shot back. "She'll have room."

"Right now she needs formula that you don't have," Becca explained. "She needs to be bottle-fed. Later she'll need approximately forty-four pounds of food a day to stay alive, but her stomach, when full, can weigh well over a hundred pounds. She'll need feedings around the clock, medicine administered, her cage cleaned. And moose get big. As they grow older, they can also become dangerous."

"She won't hurt me; she likes me. And I can give her milk from a bottle just like anyone else."

"Andy, that's enough," Sharon admonished. "You knew yesterday we couldn't keep the calf."

"But it's not fair!" He scowled, tears in his eyes. "I found her! She belongs to me!"

Becca stood from her kneeling position. "Hugh is wonderful with animals, Andy. He has over forty years' experience. His father worked with the wildlife department as a vet, and Hugh has been around wildlife ever since he was a kid. His farm has a lot of wide open space for wild animals to move around. Tourists have visited and looked at them through the fence, so I'm sure Hugh wouldn't mind if you visited the moose."

"Her name is Caramel."

Sharon's stomach clenched as she heard in Andy's voice the extent of his attachment to the animal.

"And anyways, we don't have a car, so how am I supposed to get to the farm?" Andy's words were terse.

"Maybe Jared will take you if you ask." Becca directed a brief teasing smile toward her brother-in-law, and Sharon noted his shock at her suggestion. A significant look passed between them.

"Sure, I can do that," he said looking at Andy, then Sharon.

Already feeling like a leech for intruding upon Jared's time with the next day's forced shopping trip, Sharon opened her mouth to respond. But Andy spoke first, hurling angry words at Sharon.

"You never let me have anything!" Angry tears filled his eyes. "I've always wanted a pet, but I never could have one because of Dad—and now, when I can have one, you won't let me. You hate me!"

He whirled around and sped out the door.

"Andy!" Sharon prevented herself from running after him. She knew he needed time alone, but her son's pain pierced her heart. "I'm sorry," she said in embarrassment to Jared and Becca.

"That's all right," Becca sympathized. "I understand."

"It must be tough raising kids alone," Jared added quietly.

"Lately it's been no picnic, that's for sure." Sharon attempted a weak smile his way as Becca led the moose calf to her truck. Mindy and Kitty watched with sad interest as Becca situated the animal in the back; Andy was nowhere in sight.

Before she slipped behind the wheel of her truck, Becca gave Jared a hug. "Josh and I will see you at supper this Friday?"

"Sure will," Jared agreed.

They watched as Becca drove away. The girls looked after the moose with woebegone expressions.

"I can take you to visit the moose," Jared assured.

The morose frowns evolved into grateful smiles. "Can we go tomorrow?"

"Next week might be better," Jared hedged. Though he didn't know for sure, he had a feeling Hugh would want to get the moose settled into a routine before bringing outsiders to visit.

Once he'd given his promise, the girls scrambled off, chattering about a tea party and dolls.

"You two are close," Sharon said. "You and Becca, I mean."

"Becca is like a little sister to me, though when we first met, she wanted more of a relationship."

The admission didn't surprise Sharon in the slightest. She'd seen the admiring glances Becca gave Jared.

He glanced her way. "I introduced her to one of my younger brothers, Josh, and it was love at first sight for both of them. They're a matched set."

It was on the tip of her tongue to ask why Jared hadn't been interested in Becca, who seemed pretty, intelligent, and kind, but she decided silence would serve better. She didn't need to broach a discussion on personal relationships, which could become embarrassing if it led to what happened between them in the shop yesterday.

As though he'd read her mind, his expression grew fixed. "I gave the situation over to God years ago, about me finding a wife. I haven't dated since then, and I don't plan on doing so." His eyes continued staring into hers, affecting her clear to her spine so she had trouble gaining a breath.

"Well"—the mood broke as he gave her a slight grin—"I need to get back to the farm. I'll pick you up at noon tomorrow." Sharon gave the barest of nods, and he strode away to his car. His somber words clutched her heart like a vice, and remembering his opening remark at their first meeting, she stood and watched as he drove away.

"I'm not that woman, Jared," she whispered. "I never can be."

&

Jared almost laughed at the relief that crossed Sharon's face when he arrived to pick her and her children up for their shopping trip. She hadn't really imagined he would drive a horse and wagon down the highway into the city, had she? He had told her it wasn't his regular mode of transportation; she'd seen his car. Then again, she already considered him a polite psychopath, so who knew what she thought?

They barely spoke during the twenty-minute ride, and Jared sensed Sharon had something on her mind. Noticing the friction between Andy and his mother, it didn't take a lot of speculation to determine its cause. To help ease tension, Jared turned the radio on to a Christian soft rock station and got a glimpse of Andy in the rearview mirror rolling his eyes skyward at Jared's choice. He wondered if the boy disapproved of the mild music or its message.

Once he found a parking space near the department store Sharon pointed out, he hurried around to her side of the car. She held onto the latch, her focus turned toward the backseat as she imparted last-minute instructions to her kids, and when Jared opened her door, she gave a surprised start. She eyed him with suspicion as she emerged, again ignoring his offered hand as if she suspected a practical joke, and he wondered if no man had ever opened a car door for her. . .any door for her, he thought, as he also opened the glass door of the department store and she gave him another odd look.

An elderly woman laden with bags nodded her smiling thanks as Jared kept the door open for her, as well. When he joined Sharon, she eyed him as if he were a goldfish in a birdcage.

"What?" he asked.

"Nothing." She shook her head as though unable to figure him out.

They headed toward the escalator to the second floor. An excited pair of small children raced ahead to be the first up the rising metal stairs, and Jared pulled Sharon out of their path and harm's way. She tensed and withdrew her arm from his grasp, stepping away from him at the first possible moment. He said nothing as the children's mother approached. She made a quick apology, brushed past them, and hurried to the escalator in pursuit of her young ones.

Upstairs, Sharon looked at her son. "Over in that far corner with the sailboat suspended from the ceiling is the boys' department. Your sisters and I will be over there"—she pointed to the other side of the store—"in little girls'. Like I told you earlier, Andy, now that you're older, I'm giving you more freedom by letting you choose your own clothes—but nothing with rips, tears, patches, or hems undone."

"But it's in style."

"I don't care what's in style." Her soft-spoken words brandished the rod of authority. "It's hard enough to keep you in clothes that don't unravel within weeks and that still follow the dress codes, so I don't need you choosing jeans and shirts that already have wear to them. And Andy, please make sure they cover *all* the areas they're supposed to, not just parts."

"Aw, Mom, can't I be like all the other guys? It's bad enough being the new kid on the block."

"Then save up your money and buy whatever ripped clothes you want to wear. But I won't invest in them. Are we clear on that?"

"Yeah, right, whatever."

He didn't move.

"The clothes aren't going to grow feet and walk to find you, Andy," Sharon urged.

"What about *him*?" He directed a glare Jared's way, doing nothing to hide his animosity.

"Mr. Crisp was kind enough to bring us to the mall so we could buy you clothes," she said in a quiet but firm undertone. "Please treat him with the respect due him and watch that attitude."

"Is he going with you?"

Sharon sighed. "I imagine he'll do whatever he wants to, since he's an adult and has the option of making his own decisions. You on the other hand, don't." She seemed to relent a bit. "I'll be okay. Now get hopping. I want to get home before Christmas," she exaggerated. "Be sure and stay on this level— don't go anywhere else."

Andy stomped off, and Jared wondered at her strange message to the boy, that she would be okay.

Sharon watched him go, her brow wrinkled with worry, before turning to her youngest with a smile. "Okay, Kitty, let's see what they have for you."

Jared stood in place, uncertain of what to do or where to go. Kitty looked up at him, her big blue eyes including him in their group.

"You'll come with us, too, won't you, Mr. Crisp? I really do need a man's opinion," she added.

At the six-year-old's remark, which came with all the simper and attitude of a full-grown Southern belle, Jared noticed Sharon wore the same shock that must cover his face.

"Uh, sure," he answered, and Kitty turned with a satisfied whirl of her plaid skirt. She headed the line to the girls' department, as if they, her entourage, were to follow.

"I really have no idea where she picks up these things," Sharon said from beside him. "I would guess prime-time TV; I had to work the late-night shift this past year before moving to Goosebury, and who knows what my kids watched in the babysitter's company while I was away."

Her statement bore self-condemnation, which Jared felt misplaced.

"Don't be so hard on yourself. You've done well by these kids. It's easy to tell you're a good mother and only want what's best for them."

"Thanks." She gave him a sidelong glance as if he didn't know what he was talking about. After the altercations with Andy, he understood her hesitance.

"It must be difficult to raise them without a man around to help."

He had intended his statement as sympathetic, but once he heard his words aired, he realized she could take them wrong.

She got that worried look again and darted him another glance. "Listen, you and I both know this outing was a lame attempt on your aunts' part to get us together. But let me tell you from the beginning, I'm not interested in getting married again. Ever. And that includes dating. So if that in any way interferes with your future plans—as a remark you made the other day leads me to believe—it would be best if you and I don't connect again after this shopping excursion is over. I appreciate your taking the time out of your busy schedule to bring us here, Jared, don't get me wrong, but I want to avoid any misunderstandings right from the start."

He chuckled and gave a wry shake of his head. "That was some speech. Did it take long to prepare?"

She stopped in the aisle and blinked at him in shock.

He smiled to show he was teasing. "Sharon, it's okay. Relax. I don't have ulterior motives, and if it's okay with you, I'd like to start over again and pretend our first meeting never happened. Just as friends—nothing more planned or hoped for." He didn't want a ready-made family and felt he must have been mistaken on hearing from God about Sharon being the wife for him.

He held out his hand to her. "Jared Crisp, moose catcher extraordinaire. Nice to meet you."

She let out a short laugh, glanced down at his hand, then back into his eyes. She shook his hand and released it, though the sparkle in her eyes told him she again felt at ease, perhaps for the first time that day. "Sharon Lester, overworked and underrated mom, but only one of many of my kind. It's nice meeting you, too."

"Mom, are you okay?" Mindy stood in the middle of the aisle, her expression a study of confusion. Kitty stood at one of the end-cap displays, sliding dresses and outfits over the circular rack and selecting them with all the excitement of a new starlet bearing a charge card with zero credit limits.

"You're not planning to try all those on, are you?" Sharon asked, picking up on Jared's train of thought at the humongous pile hung over Kitty's skinny arm. Numerous clothes racks stood throughout the area, which was twice the size of a tennis court. Two hangers with outfits that looked as if they were made of blue handkerchiefs slid from the pile Kitty held and to the floor by her white sneakers.

"You big dummy," Mindy said. "You're only supposed to pick from this section, in your size."

"I'm not a dummy. The sign says 6X."

"No, it says $6. Don't you even know how to read?" her sister shot back.

Kitty's brow wrinkled when she realized her mistake. In disappointment she looked at the small section of the rack Mindy motioned to, which amounted to no more than three inches width, mostly of the same outfit in the same color.

"Mindy, no name-calling. Kitty, there are plenty of clothes to choose from in your size, with a lot more racks still to look through. This is a big store." She helped her daughter hang the oversized clothes back on the rack between their proper number holders and directed a look toward Jared. "Are you sure you're up for this?"

At her impish but innocent look—the first time she'd ever relaxed around him enough to tease—he grinned. "Well, it'll be a new experience, anyway. I feel a little like Lewis and Clark on the verge of exploring a new world."

"Oh, yeah." Sharon laughed. "You have no idea."

He didn't miss the wicked twinkle in her eyes or the way her lips twitched at the corners as she turned from him. Suddenly, Jared felt a lot like that goldfish in the birdcage. . .or maybe a songbird in a goldfish bowl. He felt the strangest need to gulp down a massive supply of oxygen.

A gullible male caught in the shopping trap of a feminine clothes-world experience, that's what he was. What had he been thinking when he agreed to what surely must be every man's daymare? He couldn't call it a nightmare since the sun was still out.

"Second thoughts?" Sharon asked sweetly, catching his eye as he edged toward the aisle. Kitty squealed as she spun a second rack of dresses, whirling the poor holder around like a Looney Tunes Tasmanian Devil.

At the challenge in Sharon's eyes, he squared his shoulders and forced his shoes to stop sliding inch by inch over the flat gray carpet toward the aisle floor.

"Just lead the way, Lewis," he muttered.

"Sure thing, Clark."

Again, she gave him that all-knowing smile.

❧

Sharon could almost laugh if she didn't feel so sorry for the poor guy. Kitty was acting true to form and insisting on modeling every outfit to pirouette and gain advice. It concerned and saddened Sharon that her youngest daughter sought Jared's opinion each time. Kitty yearned for a father figure in her life; she was too young to really remember the continual threat Mark posed, and only desired what many other girls her age had—a father.

Sharon felt Kitty was too young to tell of the past she would prefer they all forget, though one day she knew she might have to. Of their family, Kitty was the only member who'd not been targeted by Mark's outbursts; she must have forgotten the nightmares that woke her, crying, during those dark days.

"What do you think of this one, Mr. Crisp?" Kitty asked with a smile, holding out the hem of the latest blue number.

"I'm beginning to feel like a potato chip as often as you girls call me that," he said. "So why don't you call me Jared instead?"

"Mom?" Both girls looked her way, and Sharon hesitated, then nodded her permission. If he didn't mind the informality, she wasn't going to insist on decorum.

"So, Jared," Kitty insisted, "you like?"

Sharon glanced to where he leaned against the counter, his stance a bit awkward. His eyes appeared to have glazed over as though his brain had turned to mush, and she hid a smile. "Maybe that's enough, Kitty. You have plenty of dresses to decide from."

"But Mom, this is *important*. I want to try out for children's choir like it said we could in the bulletin, and I have to look just perfect."

"I should think it's your voice that you'd be concerned with," Sharon said, noting Jared's sudden alert expression; the first sign he'd come back to the land of the living since Kitty had started her fashion show twenty minutes before. Andy finished his shopping in half the time, and now stood with his hands in his coat pockets, impatiently waiting for Sharon to go to the boys' department and approve his choices. To his credit, he said nothing to hurry his little sister along, but he'd always adopted favoritism with Kitty, as a protective big brother.

"Jared, do you like this blue one better or the green one?" Kitty insisted.

His shifting eyes reminded Sharon of a cornered animal. "I'm not sure I remember which is which," he admitted.

"I'll try the green one on again." Kitty headed for the dressing room.

"The yellow!" Jared called out. "The yellow was best."

"Which one? The one with flowers on the skirt or the lacey things on it?"

He looked like he might start to hyperventilate. His face went a shade red. "Uh. . .the lace?"

"I liked that one, too," Kitty said with a decisive nod. "Okay. Which shirt did you like? I can't wear a dress every day—Mama won't let me."

"Kitty," Sharon said noting the panic that had sparked to life in Jared's eyes again, "they're having a sale on the shirts. We can get all three."

"Really?" Her eyes went wide. "Yea!"

"Keep it down," she said to her daughter, but Kitty had already raced toward the dressing room.

"Thanks," Jared said, and Sharon smiled.

"Not a problem."

Andy looked back and forth between them, then bridged the distance to stand beside Sharon. "Can we get my stuff now?"

"Patience, Andy. I can't leave Kitty here by herself."

"Mindy's here."

Yeah, a lot of help she would be. Sharon looked to where her older daughter thumbed through a table display of filmy scarves, beaded bags, and other accessories.

"Five more minutes," Sharon promised.

She wished she could buy all their purchases at one register, but store policy prevented it. Or maybe something about their actions or appearance made the store clerk nervous and afraid they would shoplift, so she'd told Sharon she had to purchase the clothes in that department when it really wasn't necessary. Then again, maybe she was just being paranoid. Sharon had no way of knowing, but she did note the young girl's frequent glances in their direction.

Sharon's mind drifted back to the past, to pre-Christianity days—when her husband forced her to steal from mini marts and even stores like this one. To refuse had been to face a worse punishment than what any policeman could mete out.

"Sharon?"

She looked at Jared and tried to compose her face into a blank expression. He looked at her as though she hadn't succeeded.

"You okay?"

"Sure." She gave a careless smile and shrugged. "Just thinking."

He hesitated as if doing some of his own thinking. "I asked if you'd like to get a bite to eat after this. The mall has some good restaurants."

Sharon hedged, not sure how to respond. She knew her kids must be hungry; she was hungry. And Jared must be to have suggested a meal. But she couldn't let him pay, and she didn't dare tell him she couldn't afford a restaurant outing, not after this clothes shopping excursion.

She bit so hard on the corner of her lip she felt she'd almost bit through it. If she canceled out the weekend trips to the video rental store for a month—her one concession to paid family entertainment—she could swing lunch today.

"Mom, can I have these two scarves? Both would look really cool as a belt with my tops."

Sharon noted the cost of each of the long, embroidered, fringed accessories—one turquoise, the other black. Even on sale, their prices ranged in the two digit numbers. Already she sensed a permanent hole resided in her pocketbook, and she hadn't added in the price of the clothes Andy had selected yet.

"No." Sharon felt a twinge of pain at Mindy's hurt look. "I bought you clothes last week; this is Kitty and Andy's turn." She hated having to say no to her kids, hated their looks of disappointment even more. They had endured so much dis-illusionment and pain in their young lives. "I'm sorry, Min."

"It's okay." She shrugged but didn't make eye contact.

Sharon didn't feel as if it were okay at all; Mindy rarely asked for anything. She wished now she hadn't lashed out her answer and wondered if there was a way she could add the scarves.

"Maybe we could put them on layaway for school," Sharon suggested, knowing autumn would roll around before she knew it. Mindy's eyes grew hopeful, then clouded when Sharon questioned the salesclerk, who told them they couldn't put sale items into layaway.

She sensed Jared struggling with the idea of offering to front her the money. She had learned in her years of being married to Mark to hone in on body language. Jared straightened from the counter, intent on the conversation, his hand going to his back pocket. To avoid possible embarrassment for either of them should he offer and she would need to refuse, Sharon gave in to Mindy.

"All right. Put them with the jeans on the counter," she told her daughter. "It means no movie rentals for at least a month and a half though."

"Okay," Mindy said, too jubilant with the idea of gaining the scarves to consider future Saturday nights sans viewing entertainment.

"Did you know the local library has movies you can check out?" Jared asked. "On tape and DVD."

"Really?" Sharon and Mindy said in unison.

He nodded. "My brother's family takes advantage of it every Wednesday—you can check out up to three new releases per card and keep them for a week, free of charge."

"Thanks for letting us know." Sharon gave Jared a smile. He really wasn't such a bad guy. Now that she'd said what she needed to say, and more importantly, he'd agreed, she could relax around him and consider a simple friendship.

"I'll bet they're crummy movies," Andy muttered, shooting a glance of disinterest at Jared before looking Sharon's way.

"They have new DVD releases from as recent as this past winter. I saw that Narnia movie that's so big with kids on the shelf there, too."

"Really?" Mindy's eyes got big. "Mom?"

"We'll check it out later," she promised.

Kitty flounced out of the dressing room. "Are you sure the dress isn't too fancy to wear to choir tryouts?" she asked no one in particular, suddenly worried. "Should I pick a different dress?"

"The dress is perfect," Jared hurried to say. "But I'd save it for Sundays or special occasions. You can wear anything you want to the tryouts, Kitty. What's important is that you bring a well-rested voice."

"How would you know?" Mindy asked, her brows pulling together in curiosity.

Sharon watched Jared go a deeper shade of red. "Well, the fact of the matter is, I'm the children's new choir director—just a volunteer till they can find someone better qualified."

Everyone stared at him, no one speaking.

"Sorry, guess I should have mentioned that before."

If he had worn a tie, he would be pulling at it about now. Sharon worked to hide a smile. Suddenly, the pressure of money problems faded away. "Well, to be fair, I guess you weren't given a chance. Kitten, you heard the words from the man himself. So what say we buy what we've got and then go have some lunch?"

A rousing chorus of affirmatives met her suggestion, though Sharon knew she'd have to make a few cuts to the budget to pay for today's little over expenditure, but she figured one splurge couldn't hurt.

❧

They lunched at a café in the mall, and Jared picked up her ticket before Sharon could stop him.

"Jared, no," she said, but he'd already risen from the table and headed to the register. He sensed her lack of funds and didn't want to make things worse.

Upon his return, he confronted her grim expression with composure, waiting for the fire to fall, but it didn't. He assumed it was because her kids were there.

"I talked you into this," he explained. "It only seems right I treat."

"I don't like the idea of you buying our meals," she said in an undertone. The girls were busy discussing friends, and Andy, who had wolfed down his chicken, now frowned and picked at his chocolate cake with his fork.

"Take it as a token of our new friendship," Jared replied, wishing she wouldn't make such a big deal out of a simple gesture. "Friend to friend."

"I'm not a pauper, either." Her eyes burned into his. "I pay my debts."

"Okay." He wasn't sure what she wanted. "If you insist on returning the favor, you can pay me back by letting me take you to the library after we leave here and check out a movie I can watch with you and your kids."

Her shock matched his own. Had he really suggested such an idea? He enjoyed her company but hadn't planned on prolonging the day. Not until the words came flying from his mouth.

Andy's fork clattered to his plate. "I don't wanna see a movie. I wanna see my moose."

"It's only been a couple of days." Jared sighed at the unwanted change of subject. "I'll give Hugh a call later to find out if a visit is okay this weekend. I could take you on Saturday after my work is done at the farm."

"I want to see her now! And I don't need your permission or your ride."

"Andy," Sharon admonished. "Watch your tone, and apologize

to Jared this minute."

He turned his glare on his mother and then dropped it to his plate, offering a mumbled "sorry" to the chocolate cake.

Sharon sighed, but when she looked Jared's way, he sensed her irritation had tempered toward him by the apologetic smile she gave. "Saturday sounds good. I suppose we could make a full evening of it. Library, moose, and a movie."

His lips twitched at her witty reply. "That sounds okay by me."

Andy grunted.

"I get off work at five," Sharon said, ignoring her son's response, "so I'll have to trust you to select something decent since the library closes before then. Something family oriented that we could all watch together."

He looked at the faces around the table. The girls' eyes were bright, eager; Andy again frowned at his plate.

"Okay, I can do that. Saturday it is then."

He wondered why her words should make him feel good, especially since Andy detested the idea. All Jared sought was Sharon's friendship. . .so why was he already anticipating Saturday's approach so much?

four

Jared spent the next few days avoiding the issue, but in his quiet time with the Lord, he felt God made the matter very clear to him. He hadn't misunderstood. Sharon was the one.

"But I hadn't planned on taking on a ready-made family, Lord," he argued the first morning.

God reminded him of Joseph, who took Mary as his wife after she became pregnant.

On morning two, Jared offered another argument. "She doesn't seem to like men, especially not me, and she says she never plans on getting married."

The Lord reminded him of Hosea's story and led him to turn there. Though Gomer ran away from Hosea and to an immoral life, God urged Hosea to find her and take her back as his wife.

"Her son despises me," Jared countered the next day, though the words sounded lame.

The Lord reminded him that he hadn't chosen Andy for Jared's wife.

After three days of struggle, Jared gave in and again turned the situation completely over to God.

"Okay, Lord, if it's really Your will then You're going to have to open doors to make it happen. She slammed them all tight and padlocked them in my face. So I'll just stand back and watch You work as locksmith, if You don't mind."

At least Sharon was willing to enter into friendship with Jared and hadn't written him off as a complete psychopath due to their first meeting. As for himself, Jared felt at odds. Before he'd met her, he thought he would want a speedy engagement after long years of waiting for this moment to arrive. But now he found he didn't want to jump into anything and to take it very slow remained the best course, especially given the fact that Sharon was totally against the idea of marriage.

He felt at odds with his own goals.

Jared picked up Sharon from work on Saturday, much to her evident surprise.

"Since I was coming to your house anyway, I thought I'd swing by and spare you the walk."

"I like to walk."

Great.

"But thanks for the offer. I'll just get my purse." She offered him a doubtful smile.

Outside, when he put his fingers to her elbow to steer her to his car, she pulled away from him as if his skin were red-hot and he'd burned her.

At the question in his eyes, she explained with a feeble shrug, "I don't like being touched," then yanked open the passenger door and slid inside.

Even better.

Jared rolled his eyes heavenward and wondered if God was into practical jokes.

Didn't like being touched? Never wanted to marry again?

Like Hosea had to do with Gomer, Jared had a feeling he would need to learn and exert extreme patience with Sharon if she was part of God's plan for his life; he certainly didn't consider her promiscuous as Gomer had been, far from it. But he'd always assumed the woman God had for him would be, if not excited with the prospect of Jared as a husband, at least somewhat open to the idea. Not posting warning signals into every word or gesture or look she gave him.

The drive to her house took only a few minutes, but the

tense silence seemed to triple the time it took to get there.

She fidgeted and looked at him. "I'm sorry. About what I said back there."

He gave her a sideways glance. "Don't worry about it. My family was never much on personal space. I grew up with a lot of hugging and touching involved, so most of the time I'm not even aware I'm doing it."

She grew quiet, turning her gaze to look out the windshield, and he realized that sounded bad.

"Not meaning I touch people a lot, or that I touch just anyone—I don't." He felt his face heating. "Except for family and friends. And when I touch someone, I'm usually sincere about it."

Okay, that sounded worse.

"I mean—"

"I know what you mean." She offered him an understanding smile, getting him off the verbal hook upon which he'd impaled himself. "I grew up in a hostile environment and couldn't wait to get out of the house when I was old enough. I ran away from home and married at sixteen. I had Andy six months later. I'd just turned seventeen." She again turned her attention to the windshield. "I guess you could say I jumped right out of the frying pan and into the fire. But I didn't know it then."

Intrigued by her comment, Jared was preempted from asking more when Mindy appeared on the road, racing toward the car, Kitty far behind her.

Sharon rolled down her window. "What's wrong?" she called.

"Andy said he's going to see his moose and doesn't need Jared to take us there."

Sharon's mouth tensed. "A ten-mile walk is not something I'm going to attempt after a full day on my feet; I'll talk to him."

"But Mama, he already left."

"When?"

"Five minutes ago," Mindy rushed to say as a breathless

Kitty finally joined her. "After his cartoons were over."

"Get in the car," Jared said, sure Sharon wouldn't want to detour to her house. "We'll catch up to him."

The girls piled into the backseat. Once they buckled themselves in, Jared took off. They soon spotted Andy. Jared pulled closer to where the boy walked alongside the road and eased his foot off the accelerator.

"Get in the car, Andy," Sharon said out the open window, her tone brooking no refusal.

Andy tensed and faced her off as Jared hit the brakes. The boy seemed about to argue, but something in his mom's expression must have stopped him. He did as she said, slamming the door harder than necessary.

And now off to begin this fun outing.

Somehow Jared didn't think a medley of car tunes would help ease the tension this time.

❧

Sharon had just about had it with her son; there was no excuse for his surly behavior. Once they reached Hugh MacFarland's farm, Andy took off running to the chain fence.

"Andy, wait!"

He refused to listen and twined his fingers through the iron links as he scanned the area.

A strapping giant of a man with gray hair and crinkles around his eyes came from a building outside the gate to greet them.

First he shook Jared's hand. "Nice to finally meet you. Becca talks a lot about her 'big brother.' She explained the situation, and while I don't normally allow visits at this stage, I decided to make an exception for the boy." He looked at Sharon and the two girls, his confusion evident.

"I'm sorry. Andy is really eager to see the moose," Sharon said, motioning behind her to where Andy stood at the fence. "I'm Sharon Lester, and these are my daughters, Mindy and Kitty."

Hugh gave them all a welcoming smile. "All right then." He led them toward the fence where Andy stood. After introducing himself, he explained to Andy in a firm but gentle voice, "I prefer as little human interaction with the moose calf as possible. But you're welcome to watch her through the protective fence."

Andy nodded, though he didn't appear happy. Sharon gave him a warning look, and he gave a little quirk of his mouth. "Thank you, sir."

"Sure. Well, come along then. I hear you're eager to see her." He led them to another enclosed area, this one smaller and cut off from where other animals roamed.

As they approached, Sharon saw the baby moose drinking from a bottle hooked to the fence.

"Wow, she's gotten big," Andy said, his surliness forgotten.

"She sure has. She looks like she's weeks older and not days," Sharon added.

"Moose grow very fast," Hugh said. "We still hope to release her to the wild at some point, though she wouldn't take the bottle at first and had to be hand fed. She's young enough that we hope it won't present a problem."

At the sound of their voices, the moose stopped feeding and turned her head to look at them.

"Here, Caramel." Andy's fingers wiggled through the fence. "Here, girl."

"Andy, don't," Sharon warned under her breath.

The moose looked Andy's way and pricked its ears.

"Can I pet her?" He turned hopeful eyes toward Hugh.

"Andy, you heard what he said about human interaction."

"Please?" He ignored his mom, his eyes still on Hugh. "We're friends. She knows me."

"I'm not so sure, Andy. Moose—or any wild animal for that matter—don't tend to be friendly or trust—"

The moose warily picked its way toward them and stopped at the fence between Andy and Jared.

"Well, I'll be. . ." Hugh's words trailed off.

"Maybe she wants you to sing to her again, Jared," Mindy said, and Sharon noted the embarrassment on his face.

The moose craned its neck to sniff at Andy's fingers. Its tongue came out to lick once, before it stepped back.

"She's thanking you, Andy," Kitty squealed in delight.

Hugh didn't look as pleased. Yet when Andy glanced his way, he managed a smile. "Looks like you did make a friend."

"So can I pet her?"

"I'd rather you didn't. It's for her sake, son. Too much human interaction can make her dangerous and unfit to release in the wild."

"At petting zoos they let us pet the animals," Mindy argued, not helping matters any.

"Yes, but those animals will never again be released to the wild. They'll live out their existence in a zoo, always dependant upon people to give them food and never able to learn to forage on their own."

"Elsa did," Mindy argued. "So why can't Caramel?"

"Elsa?"

"The lion in the *Born Free* movie. They had her for a pet, then released her."

"Ah, Elsa. Of course." Hugh's mouth twitched, and Sharon wondered if he had children of his own to be so patient with hers. "That was a vastly different situation. The owners understood wildlife, and though I don't remember the movie to the letter, it seems to me as if they encountered a great number of problems reacquainting Elsa to the wilds of Africa. She almost died before they were successful. Wildlife, for the most part, just aren't meant to become house pets. Animals of the wild were created to know and live the life God meant for them to have."

His answer seemed to pacify the children, though none of them looked happy. Sharon had never been able to give them a pet; her husband wouldn't allow one, and then when she and the children lived on their own, the apartment they rented had a no-pets policy. She wondered if the sisters would mind if she bought the children a dog or a cat.

They remained twenty minutes longer, neither Andy nor Mindy wanting to leave. At Sharon's lure that Jared had checked out a movie for them to watch, both Kitty and Mindy were ready to go, but it took some prodding to pull Andy from the fence. Rather than order him to come, Sharon cajoled him, saying they were having his favorite that night—creamy chicken Alfredo.

Andy looked at Hugh. "Can I come back and visit her again?"

At first Sharon thought the man might refuse, and who could blame him, but instead he gave a kind nod. "Sure. As long as you follow my rules, I don't mind your visiting. I have other animals on my farm, as you no doubt noticed. Goats, calves, rabbits, a few dogs, and several cats. You're welcome to visit with them, too. Some would enjoy the company and the attention, and you can pet most of them at will."

"Can we, Mama?" Mindy turned eager eyes her way.

"Well, I don't see why not."

"Will you bring us again, Jared?" Mindy asked, giving Sharon a turn at blushing. She didn't want him to think they assumed him to be their permanent personal chauffeur, which was how it was beginning to look.

He glanced at Sharon as if reading her mind and grinned. "Sure, I'd love to."

Andy stalked off to the car without another word.

five

Jared never thought he would hear Sharon squeal like a little girl. The shine in her eyes and the glow of her face made him glad he'd chosen this movie and not the other one about toys that came to life. The Narnia one had been checked out.

"I take it you approve?" he asked with a grin.

"I haven't seen this movie since I was a kid. When I was a little girl, I used to dream Chitty was my car and would take me places far away, like 'Hushabye Mountain'—to happy places where all was safe."

Her wistful words seemed to cover a great deal more, and Jared felt as if an invisible fist closed around his heart.

From behind Sharon, Andy glanced at the cover of the Disney DVD she held. "It looks stupid. And what a dumb title: *Chitty Chitty Bang Bang*. Who thought up something retarded like that?"

Even her son's taunts didn't wipe the smile from Sharon's face. "Don't knock it till you've tried it, champ."

They'd enjoyed a reasonably friendly supper—at least Andy didn't glare at Jared from across the table the entire time. He had been too busy gulping down the delicious meal Sharon had prepared. Jared hoped the boy's animosity toward him wouldn't spark up again, now that they had consumed the last of the apple pie.

By the time the actor who played Caractacus Potts had gone to the candy factory with his invention, the children, including Andy, were absorbed in the story. Even Sharon sat like a child, a delighted smile on her face. Andy sat between them—he had plunked himself in the middle cushion the moment Sharon sat down. Jared realized it was Andy's way of putting distance between Sharon and Jared.

"It would be so neat to make candy." Kitty's expression grew wistful as she lay stretched out in front of the TV, her chin propped on her hands.

"We do that very thing at my family's farm," Jared said.

"Really?" Kitty turned wide eyes his way.

"Sure do. Maple sugar candies. I usually have some hard candy on me, but today I don't. I'll bring you a sample next time I see you."

"Sh!" Andy said. "I'm trying to watch the movie."

Jared caught Sharon's apologetic look on her son's behalf but wasn't surprised at the youth's curt remark. The boy had labeled him an enemy from the start, and by the manner in which he always seemed to insert himself between Sharon and Jared, whether by words or actions, it wasn't difficult to figure out why.

The movie ended with a rousing sing-along of the theme song, which both girls began to croon, and Jared thought he heard Sharon hum. But Kitty hadn't forgotten Jared's previous comment.

"Do you really own a factory and make candy?"

"Well, not a factory like in the movie, no, but we do have a building set aside with workers—most of them family members—who boil and prepare the syrup, getting it ready for distribution. From the syrup we make candy using a family recipe."

"Wow." Kitty's eyes sparkled.

"Neatness," Mindy added.

"Do you know where maple syrup comes from, Kitty?" he asked.

She thought hard. "From cans?"

Andy laughed, and Sharon shot him a mild warning glance. He quieted and smiled at his sister with friendly tolerance, putting out his hand to tousle her hair. He seemed to have a strong tie to both his sisters.

"Well, to begin with, no," Jared said. "But it does wind up in tins. It comes from inside trees."

He didn't think it possible for her huge eyes to go wider. "Trees?"

Jared nodded. "Maple trees. We tap the trees in the springtime, capturing the sap, and then boil it to make syrup. We travel by horse and wagon to collect the sap from the buckets of those trees within easy reach, in what we call gathering."

"Wow, that's so cool," Mindy said.

"You don't use a tractor?" Andy asked.

"No, our family holds to old-fashioned ideals whenever possible. Tourists love the horse and wagon bit, and we even put a picture of Tamany on the cans."

"Really? I want to see!" Kitty shot like a cannonball for the kitchen. Soon creaks and slams of cabinets flying open followed.

"Kitty, don't wreck the place," Sharon called in alarm. "We ran out of syrup yesterday, and I threw the tin away already."

"I'll bring some of that next time I come, too," Jared promised.

"We don't need any of your lousy syrup," Andy said. "It's awful."

Mindy rolled her eyes and ran to the kitchen.

"Andy!" Sharon stared in shock at her son. "Apologize to Jared."

"Because I don't like his stinking syrup?"

"No, because that's not how you treat a guest, and with the way you wallowed your French toast in syrup at breakfast yesterday, I should think you like his syrup very well. It's because of you we ran out of it."

Andy scowled. "I'm going to my room."

Before Sharon could say another word, he pivoted on his heel and stormed down the hall. She seemed to wither as Jared watched her.

"I'm sorry about all that." She glanced at him.

"It's okay; I understand. He feels like I'm a threat."

Her eyes seemed to sharpen with comprehension at his comment, and she cast a nervous look toward the kitchen, where both girls were.

"Can you stay for coffee? I know it's late, but I think explanations are in order. I have to get the girls to bed first, and I don't want them to hear what I have to say."

"Sure." He felt cheered that she wanted him to extend his visit for whatever reason. "Want me to start the percolator?"

"If you'd like. It takes about a half hour for their baths; they like to play in the bubbles. But I can cut playtime shorter. Then there are bedtime prayers. Often Kitty requests a story afterward, but they can do without a story for one night."

"No, you do whatever it is you usually do. Don't cut things short on my account."

Her expression softened with something like wonder before she turned away. "You know where the kitchen is. Let them know Mom said it's bedtime." She said the last a little more loudly.

Jared watched her disappear down the hallway and into what he assumed was the bathroom before he entered the kitchen.

Mindy rolled her eyes and grinned. "We heard." She shot a look to her sister. "I get dibs on Mr. Suds," she said and ran out of the room.

"No fair! You had him last time." Kitty chased after her sister.

Jared chuckled, wondering why children always felt the need to run and where they got such energy. Sharon's children were beyond energetic; around them, he felt his years, even if they were only in the tri-decade. Again, he wondered if he had what it took to tackle such a feat. Most men started a family from scratch; he would get the full deal all at once.

God, if this really is Your plan, then You're going to need to equip me to be the kind of man they need in their lives.

Jared easily found the coffee and went about making it. The rich aroma permeated the kitchen by the time Sharon made an appearance. She seemed a little flustered.

"Everything okay?"

"Yes, they flew through their bath in record time. Really strange." She seemed preoccupied, worried. "They asked me to ask you something."

He lifted his brows, waiting.

"They want you to read them their story tonight."

"Oh." Jared hadn't expected that. He stood up from the table. "Do you mind?"

She shrugged as if she didn't care either way, but the troubled look in her eyes didn't match her supposed indifference.

≈

Sharon stood in the doorway of the girls' room and watched as Jared sat on Kitty's bed, a book in his large hands. Both girls sat on either side of him and cozied up to him as though he were their father. Kitty propped her elbow on his leg, leaning in to him, and Mindy craned close as though interested in the opposite page.

A sharp twinge pulled at Sharon's heart. They had never known the love of a father, though since she'd become a Christian over three years ago, she'd been trying to teach them about the love of their heavenly Father. Still, for two little girls not yet at an age to understand so much about life and death, or even about God, she knew it wasn't always enough to be told they had the affection of an invisible being.

They wanted visible arms of strength to hold them, an audible voice to comfort and assure protection in a way only a father could. She shared the girls' dilemma; she'd never known the love of an earthly father. Her birth father had died before Sharon was born, and her stepfather had been a beast; her mother too troubled with her own worries to care about the needs of her two girls. In all honesty, at times Sharon still felt disassociated from the world, and so very lonely. Lonely enough to yearn for a pair of strong, gentle arms to hold and comfort her, too.

She listened to Jared's low, soothing voice as he read the silly story of a ladybug and a grasshopper, one that Mindy had long outgrown but now responded to with smiles and giggles as if it had been her choice.

Once he closed the book, the girls made it clear they weren't ready to let him go just yet.

"Tell us how you make candy," Kitty implored.

"And how you get the syrup out of the trees," Mindy added.

"Do you use straws?"

"Do you saw the trees in half?"

Under their sudden and fervent stream of questions, Jared looked a little taken aback. He caught sight of Sharon and gave a lopsided "how'd I get into this?" grin.

"Tell you what. Next spring, when it's sugaring time—what we call the time to collect syrup from the sugar bush, the maple trees—how about if I take you to the farm and show you how it's done?"

Kitty squealed. "Really? You mean we get to ride in the wagon with Tamany?"

"Well, Tamany will be leading it," Jared corrected, amused.

"Honest?" Mindy asked.

"If it's okay with your mom." All three looked at Sharon

with pleading expressions. But a mischievous smile lifted Jared's mouth, and she detected a twinkle in his eyes, too.

He knew what position he'd placed her in. She should be irritated that he would force her to make such a decision in front of the girls. How could she say no when they looked at her with such big, pleading eyes, like little kittens in their white, fuzzy robes? Yet how could she say yes, when further attachment to Jared could only hurt them since he could never be the father figure they clearly expected? With a slight smile and an even slighter shake of her head, she narrowed her eyes, promising him a future reckoning.

"That's still pretty far in the future to make plans about now," she said at last.

"I know, I know," Mindy replied. "Live each day that comes without wondering or worrying what the future has in store."

The flip way Mindy spouted the mantra that Sharon had clung to and repeated during the most horrific days of her life made her feel a little sick inside. She glanced away, unable to look in their eyes as she tucked her daughters into their beds and kissed them good night. She sensed Jared watch her as he stood to the side the entire time.

Once she flicked the light switch and closed the door, he again looked at her. "You okay?"

"Sure. I just need to say good night to Andy. Go ahead and pour us some coffee—if you don't mind?"

"Of course not." He moved down the hallway, and Sharon watched him a moment before heading to her son's room. She tapped on the door. When he didn't answer, she nudged it open a few inches.

"Andy?"

Paying no attention to her, he sat on the bed, his back to her as he thumbed through a comic book. So that was how it was going to be.

She approached him. "I'm not going to get into a big reci-tation of what you did wrong out there—you already know. But what I want to know is why you're acting this way." She sat next to him, putting her hand on his shoulder. "What's bothering you, son?"

Her gentleness broke Andy, and he bowed his head, trying hard not to cry, then burrowed his head against her shoulder.

"I'm sorry, Mom. I just don't want him here. Why did he have to come, anyway?"

His answer confirmed her suspicions. "We're just friends, Andy. Nothing else. Everyone needs friends, and Jared is a nice guy." With the words aired, she realized how true they were.

"Yeah?" He pulled back and eyed her with suspicious anger. "And how long'll that last? How long till he hurts you like Dad did?"

His words made her wince. Not for herself, but for her son. "Andy, not all men are like your father—"

"You said Dad was nice, too, when you first met. That's what you told us."

Sharon drew a sharp breath. She'd been fooled by Mark's charm and sweet talk, but their marriage hadn't been bad until he mixed with the wrong crowd after losing his job. He'd started taking drugs and drinking more heavily.

"What do you want me to do, Andy?" She withdrew her arm from around his shoulder and studied his face. "You want me to be without friends?"

"You have us."

She hugged him to her again. "Yes, I do. And I love you guys bunches. But you're my children; when I say friends, I mean adult friends."

"What about Leslie and Jill and Carly?"

"You're right. They're my friends, and I'm thankful for

them. But they're also married women with lives of their own and new babies to take care of, besides. Babies are wonderful blessings from God, but they can be a handful and take a lot of a mother's time. I talk to Leslie and the others on the phone and see them at church, and that's great. But sometimes I enjoy having someone my age to hang with, too."

At first, it hadn't mattered; her children were everything to her and still were. But in the last year, Sharon had begun to feel the loneliness sharpen and produce within her a strong desire for adult companionship.

He scowled. "Like Mr. Crisp."

Sharon sighed. "Jared has shown our family nothing but kindness, Andy. Taking time out of his life to help us, to drive us where we needed to go, even helping to save the moose calf." It was the wrong thing to say.

"It's because of him I lost her!" Andy shot back, his eyes burning with hatred again. "If he hadn't called his stupid sister-in-law, then she would've never taken Caramel away."

"That's enough, Andy." Sharon rose from the bed. "We did what was right and what was lawful. We've talked about this before, and you know how I feel. End of story." She bent and kissed his brow, but he didn't respond. "Lights out. Tomorrow is another day, and it'll be here before you know it."

She exited the room, turning back at the door to see him sitting in the same position. Sighing, she clicked off the wall switch, leaving him in the glow of his bedside lamp, and shut the door.

Their conversation escalated her agitation coming so soon after watching the happy picture of Jared with her girls. As she walked into the kitchen, Sharon reached a decision, one made no easier with the friendly smile Jared beamed her way.

six

Jared knew something was wrong when Sharon didn't return his smile. She seemed edgy again, offering him only a fleeting look before heading to the cupboard to pull out a box of powdered sugar doughnuts.

"Want some?" she asked.

"Sure. I poured the coffee," he added unnecessarily, since she had already seen the mugs.

"Thanks." She set the box on the table between them. "I'm sorry I only have prepared foods to offer you. I don't cook meals from scratch anymore."

"Do you hear me complaining?" He studied her, puzzled. "As long as it's good, I'm happy. And the meal was great."

Still, she seemed distant as she pulled a doughnut from the box, dunking it in her black coffee. Jared did likewise with his sugared coffee, then wished he hadn't once he took a sip; the powdered sugar made the coffee too sweet. He took another sip anyway, trying not to wince.

Sharon's mouth twitched. "You don't have to drink it, Jared. I can get you a fresh cup."

Before she could take away his coffee, he wrapped his fingers around the handle. "It's all right."

"I know it's not the best coffee, but it was on sale—"

"Sharon." He set his mug down. "Will you please stop apologizing? There's no reason to."

She seemed surprised by his gentle request and looked into her mug a moment. He wondered if she always beat herself up over inconsequential matters.

"About Andy. . .again, I want to apologize for his behavior. To understand what's going on with him, you'd have to know what he's been through these past few years." She ran her finger along the inside loop of the mug's handle, her eyes intent on her action. "My husband died in prison. He attacked a woman—a friend of mine now, actually—who writes a local advice column. Mark arranged a meeting with her in a park a few towns away and stabbed her there."

Jared sat still, dreading what was coming but, at the same time, needing to hear it.

"I'd written her for advice. Mark found out and. . .well, let's just say he wasn't happy. Things came to a head, and I left with the kids. He pretended to be me, to lure Dear Granny to the park—that's the pseudonym she uses for the column. To honor a promise, I can't tell you her real name, though you probably know her. Anyway, I called the police when I read the newspaper account and realized it had to be Mark. He was convicted and sent to prison for his crimes, which included not only attempted homicide, but also possession of narcotics, firearms, and a few other tidbits the police found when they searched the house. I wasn't there; I'd gotten away from him long before that."

Jared briefly closed his eyes and swallowed. Things were falling into place.

"I visited him in prison, though. He was still my husband, and I was raised to believe that you don't just ditch a marriage. More than anything, I wanted Mark to change. Those last years with him, when things got bad, I kept hoping he would, but it never happened. Each time, he promised he would, but he never did."

Her words came fast as if she needed to get them out before she lost her nerve. "I visited him twice a month for almost five years. But it was the strangest thing—a Christian ministry also visited the prison and brought literature, books, and magazines. One of the cons even headed a Bible study. He persuaded Mark to join—they were cellmates—but it took awhile before Mark agreed to try it. I'd talked to him about God, too; I was a new Christian at the time, thanks to Dear Granny." She smiled secretively. "And I wanted my husband to find Christ. Despite all he'd put us through, I didn't want him to burn in hell. And I knew he was fast headed in that direction."

She shook her head, giving a small, humorless chuckle. "The irony of all this is that he *did* come to accept Christ through his cellmate. And during that last year I saw a real change. I began to hope life could be different for us, even though he'd be in prison a long time. Next thing I know, I get a phone call about a prison fight and that Mark got stabbed. I talked to his cellmate after I collected his personal items, and he told me Mark had nothing to do with the outbreak but was just at the wrong place at the wrong time. That the last thing he whispered before he died was to let me know how sorry he was and that he loved me and the kids."

Sharon swiped at her eyes with an impatient, brisk motion. "Sorry. I promised myself I wouldn't do that." She cleared her throat. "Anyway, Mark died last year, and Andy is still dealing with hard issues concerning all of it. At this point, he resents male interference. He's been the little man of the family ever since I left Mark. A daunting responsibility for such a young boy but I never expected him to do that. He took on that responsibility himself."

Jared wanted to respond with sensitivity, but a probing question intruded. "Did your husband, did he. . ."

"Hit me?" she asked when his words trailed off. At his brusque nod, she took another sip of coffee. "Yes, when things got bad after he lost his job. I used to not be able to talk about it; that I can shows progress."

Her slight smile hinted at an undergirding of strength. "I attended a Christian-based support group for abused wives, even before Mark went to prison. Through that, I've learned some things. Among them, that I don't deserve to be a punching bag to anyone, that God made me, that He loves me, and that I'm important to Him. In the past two years, I've begun to heal and have grown closer to the Lord. I've put the past behind me and moved forward, but for the kids, it's harder. I left the very day Mark started taking out his anger on them, so they didn't get a lot of it. But Andy is the oldest, and he remembers. Everything. Mindy, I'm not sure sometimes what she's thinking, and Kitty was only a baby. But now and then with the things she says, I think she must remember something."

Sharon bowed her head and shook it. "I can steer them in the right direction, but that's it. I can't force anything—either their forgiveness of their dad or for them to let go of the pain and the past."

Jared nodded, thinking how much she'd taken on her shoulders. "When we met, I thought you were a good mother. . ."

Sharon's head jerked up, as if she expected a verbal blow, and he wondered if she received criticism from others for the decisions she'd made.

"Now I know you're a superior one."

She went a shade of rose, and with the way she averted her eyes, he knew he'd embarrassed her with his praise. "I'm glad you feel that way, Jared. It makes what I have to say a little easier."

Jared tensed.

"I have to keep my daughters' best interests in mind, and I've seen some things that disturb me." She fiddled with her doughnut, dunking it but not eating it. "They've become attached to you, in such a short time. That worries me, because I think. . ." Her dunks became more frequent, her doughnut smaller as sodden chunks fell away; still she didn't meet his gaze. "I think they expect more to come from this association than will happen. And I don't want them hurt." Her eyes lifted to his. "You understand my position, don't you?"

"I'm trying to." Jared watched her closely. "So you think we should talk to them? Explain things?" He had numerous nieces and nephews but didn't really know the first thing when it came to dealing with children.

"Actually. . ." She looked down at her coffee again. "I think it would be better if we just stop this before they get hurt."

"Stop this?" Jared didn't look away from her. "You mean stop seeing each other?"

"You make it sound like a whole lot more than it is," Sharon accused, and Jared looked down, acknowledging the truth of what she'd said. "This was supposed to be all about friendship, Jared. Nothing more."

"You're right. I'm sorry. That came out wrong."

God had told him one thing; Sharon told him another. Free will had everything to do with a person's future. He couldn't force Sharon to change her mind; he wasn't that type of person.

"So since we hardly know each other," she continued, "and since upon knowing each other, things haven't always worked out well. . ." Her words trailed off, and he knew she meant Andy. "I think it best if we just keep our distance from now on."

"That sounds almost hostile."

Her eyes flicked up, and in them he saw what looked like disappointment. For the first time he realized her pain and also the surprising hurt he felt.

"Sorry, I didn't mean to come across as sounding obstinate," he amended. "I don't want to make waves in your family, Sharon. Not when you're working so hard to make things right again. So I'll get out of your hair." Now that she'd made her wishes known, he felt like an intruder. He scooted his chair back from the table.

"You're leaving?"

The plaintive surprise in her voice shocked him. She averted her gaze a moment as though flustered by what she'd said.

"I mean, you don't have to go right now. Since you're already here and all."

"Suddenly I don't feel much like talking." He tempered his stiff words with a semismile. "Supper was great. You're an excellent cook, and I had a good time. I'll leave the movie here. The kids may want to watch it again. I know my nieces and nephews are like that. It's due back a week from today."

Sharon's expression remained troubled. "Thank you."

"Not a problem." He forced himself to relax. She couldn't help the way she felt; she only put her kids first, like any good mother. He wondered if she ever took the time to think about herself. "Take care of yourself, Sharon." He hesitated then held out his hand for her to shake.

She looked at it a moment, and too late he recalled that she didn't like being touched. That made sense now, too. But before he could pull his hand away, she placed her hand inside his.

Her hand was soft, warm, and Jared wished he could hold it forever. She didn't withdraw as quickly as she'd done on previous occasions, seeming hesitant to break contact with him.

Their eyes met, but before Jared could do something he would regret, he slid his fingers away. She began to rise from her chair, but he shook his head. "No need to walk me to the door. Finish your coffee."

Before he left the kitchen, he cast one last glance over his shoulder, noting she had barely moved and still stared into her mug. As he reached for the door, he sensed she had turned to watch him, but this time he didn't look back.

❧

"You look awful," Carly said to Sharon, as she jiggled her baby daughter, Mali, who fussed in her mother's arms.

"Carly's right, luv," Jill intoned in her Australian accent. "You don't look as if you've been getting enough sleep." Her own daughter, Jolene, napped in the shaded stroller in a frog-like position that made Sharon wonder how babies didn't get cricks in their necks.

Sharon eyed her friends with a grimace. "Wow. Thanks." She turned to Leslie. "Anything to add to the collection of compliments?"

Leslie laughed. Paula played with a doll rattle on her mom's lap as the four women sat on a bench outside the ball park, one of the rare moments they'd forged to get together for a day out, even if it included their children. The mild, sunny weather had been perfect for their noonday picnic.

"I'm worried about Andy," Sharon admitted, watching her son toss a softball around the field with Kitty and Mindy. The three played with caution around the younger children—Leslie's girl, Marena, and Jill's boy, Titus, who chased like an excited puppy after the softballs that outstretched gloves missed.

"What's the matter with Andy?" Leslie studied him. "I hadn't noticed anything."

"I don't think he's taking everything that happened with Mark well."

"Who would?" Leslie sympathized. "It's a lot for a boy his age to handle. For anyone to handle."

"I know, but it's more than that." Sharon sighed and shifted position, propping her heels on the bench with her arms around her legs. "He's become entirely too protective of me—which is strange, since we've been arguing lately and he's so angry with me. Especially about that moose calf."

"The one Jared captured with a song?" Carly asked with a chuckle.

"Yeah." Word had leaked out about the moose calf's containment, though not from Sharon, and now Jared singing to the moose was the town's latest joke.

Besides spotting him at church from a distance, Sharon had rarely seen him in the two months since they'd said good-bye, but she noticed he took the ribbing very well. More than one local had teased him about serenading the moose calf. He and Sharon made brief eye contact—no more than a nod in greeting—but she'd felt his gaze clear down her spine. On those occasions, her breath caught, and she'd quickly focused her attention on something else. Or had tried to.

Carly leaned over and looked at her a little too intently. Mali's head rested on her mom's shoulder, her huge dark eyes observing Sharon as Carly patted her back.

"It wouldn't be just Andy you're upset about, would it?"

"Well, Mindy and Kitty have been moping around the house, too." But she knew the cause for their doldrums. They missed Jared and told her so at every opportunity. His presence did seem to brighten a room, as lighthearted and funny as he could be.

"Hmm. What about you?"

"What about me?"

"Have you been moping?"

"Why should I be moping?" Sharon felt herself getting defensive.

"Why, indeed?"

Carly's smile made her uneasy, and she averted her gaze to watch the kids toss the ball.

"I hear Jared is teaching both of the girls in choir this year," Carly said after a moment.

At her words, Sharon almost snapped her neck with how fast she turned it. "Along with ten other children, yes, he is. He volunteered till someone else comes along." Too much; she'd said too much, and Jill's surprised glance in her direction told her so.

"You spoke with him about it?" Carly pursued.

"We, um, spent a couple of days together awhile back." At their intent expressions, she hastily added, "His aunts offered his services to drive me and the kids around on errands."

"Oh." Carly seemed disappointed. "I thought you meant like a date."

Sharon's face warmed at the memory of inviting him to supper. She and Jared knew she had made the offer in friendship, but her friends would see it differently. "No, not a date. I don't date."

"Too right," Jill said. "And neither does he."

"I know; he told me."

Carly's eyes widened.

Stupid thing to say, Sharon. Really stupid.

"You talked about his love life—or rather his decision to go without one?" Carly asked. "That conversation must have gotten rather personal."

Sharon slid her feet to the ground and rubbed her hand down her jeans, uneasy. "He told me about waiting for the woman God handpicked for him—after I said I wanted to keep our relationship friends-only." Her face reddened more as Jill's mouth dropped open. Leslie also stared.

"Meaning I warned him in advance, before he got it into his head that anything could go further—but this was before I knew about his feelings on dating." She didn't dare tell them what Jared had blurted out the moment he saw her. She hadn't been able to get that first meeting out of her mind. "You know how I feel about all this; I've told you I never plan to marry again. So. . ." She attempted a bright smile. "Can we just change the subject? Carly, you never did tell me how that book deal went down."

Carly hesitated as if she might pursue the topic, then shrugged. "I'm not sure yet, but the editor seemed interested in seeing more. *A Short Guide to the Long Trail* might just find a home after all."

"How does Nate feel about it?" Sharon asked, relieved that the spotlight was off her.

"He's already debating on whether we'll buy a summer beach house in Hawaii or a small chalet in Switzerland." Carly rolled her eyes and laughed. "I tried to explain that the career of a writer and bars of bullion don't necessarily go hand in hand. But he says he has faith in me, obviously more than I have in myself."

"I'm glad things have settled down for him and his family," Leslie said. "He deserves a vacation to both places. Blaine and I were talking the other night, and we think it just isn't right for a community to show hard feelings toward an innocent relative of a convicted criminal, no matter the situation."

Of the three women, Sharon felt closest to and admired Leslie the most. Sharon's husband had stabbed Leslie in the park upon learning she was the advice columnist, Dear Granny. Since Sharon had met her to apologize on the day of Leslie's discharge from the hospital, the two women had grown close, and Leslie had been the one to lead Sharon to the Lord.

"I agree," Carly said. "Things have quieted down since Nate's stepbrother was convicted. But I'm really thankful to be living in Goosebury and not in Nate's hometown, so Nate doesn't have to deal with any of the flack there; his dad wrote that some in town still treat them badly, though Nate's stepbrother was sent to prison for his crimes."

At the word prison, something tightened inside Sharon, and Carly drew her brows together. "Sorry. That was a bad slip."

"It's okay." Sharon shrugged. "It's been over half a year."

Several seconds of uneasy silence passed before Jill spoke. "I seem to remember once, Carly me mate, when you were quite fed up with your hometown and ready to fly the coop."

Carly let out a sheepish laugh. "Yeah, well, that was before I found you guys. And before my dad and I got to know one another. And before I met Nate, and he moved up here. Life has taken a definite upswing since those days. And in ways I never imagined." She peered down at Mali's rosy face. The baby slept, content on her mama's shoulder. "Even my aunt has softened around the edges with Mali's arrival."

"And who could blame her? Mali's a little gem," Leslie said.

Something clutched Sharon's heart as she looked at the sleeping baby, who had both her mama's eyes and thick black hair. Sharon had never had the big, happy family she'd envisioned, but she didn't dare go too far down that trail of thought. She had miscarried her fourth child months after Mark's arrest, and though years had passed since that time, the loss still stung.

They talked fifteen minutes longer about home, husbands, children, and work before Leslie said she had to go. The others also needed to get home for one reason or another, and Sharon's own laundry awaited, as well as the recent lists of school supplies she'd received. She couldn't believe summer was almost over and the kids would be back in school within two weeks. For her children, it would be a new adventure, a new school, and again she worried about Andy. He had become so withdrawn and somber. She had thought at Jared's absence Andy would have perked up, but that hadn't happened.

"You know I'm here for you, right?" Once she'd buckled the still-sleeping Paula into her infant seat, Leslie turned to Sharon, who stood between their cars. "Any time you need to talk, just pick up the phone. I miss having you for a neighbor."

"Me, too. But I needed something within walking distance of my job and a bigger place, especially since Andy needs his own room now. I can't believe he's almost a teenager."

"You could still call."

"What with your answering all your readers in your column and taking care of your family, I didn't want to intrude with my problems."

"It wouldn't be an intrusion, Sharon. I still make a habit of getting together with Nana on Tuesdays to sort through the reader mail, but even Dear Granny needs a break." She winked at the use of the moniker that she and her nana cowrote under. "I wish you would join us for the Bible study at Jill's."

"If I had a car, I would. It's my next planned purchase. But I can't borrow Loretta and Josephine's car on Wednesdays because they go out for bingo night."

"Blaine is putting our car in the shop, and we're hitching a ride with Carly." Leslie thought a moment. "Did you ask her for a lift? They just bought that minivan."

"I don't want to be a pain. I still don't know her that well to ask for favors."

"Are you kidding? Carly thinks you're great. Believe me, she doesn't think of you as a pain. Do you want to go next week or not?"

"Well, yes, but—"

Before Sharon realized what Leslie had in mind, her friend called across the parking lot. "Carly! Can you give Sharon a lift to Jill's house Wednesday night?"

"Leslie!" Sharon argued under her breath.

"Sure," Carly shot back with a smile. "The more the merrier."

"See how easy that was?" Leslie's eyes twinkled as she turned back to Sharon. "Though her clichés sometimes get a little hard to take." She grinned. "To be fair, she comes up with some original lines, too."

"I think Carly's and Jill's gung ho attitudes have rubbed off on you."

"I hope you're not upset?" Leslie's smile faded. "It's just that we both know you need Christian fellowship outside of church, and I've been wanting to get you over there for some time. We make a regular party of it, you know. After Bible study, we talk, eat, even shoot pool. The girls against the guys."

"I haven't shot a game of pool since Mark and I were dating," Sharon mused.

"Then you play? Great!"

"Well, I am a bit rusty." Sharon laughed.

"I'm sure you'll pick it up again in no time."

"Mom?" Kitty impatiently called from the rolled-down window. "Are we going soon?"

"I'll let you get back to your kids," Leslie said with a grin. "And I need to get home, too. Blaine gets off work early today, and I don't want him coming home to an empty house. See you on Wednesday night!"

"Okay." Sharon slid behind the wheel of the Loretta and Josephine's car.

"Are we going to Jill's?" Mindy asked before Sharon had a chance to slip the key into the ignition.

My, what big ears we have, she thought with a wry shake of her head.

"I'm going this Wednesday night, but you'll stay with a babysitter."

"Aw, Mom," Kitty said.

"Will anyone else be there?" Andy asked from the front seat.

Sharon darted a look his way, noting his intent expression. "Yes, since it's a Bible study I'm sure other people will be there."

She didn't elaborate, though she felt she knew to whom her son referred. But Jared must not be one of the regulars, or Leslie would have said so.

♥

"Hey, buddy," Nate said as he came up to Jared and slapped him on the back. "Been serenading any sweet moosies lately?"

"Funny," Jared said without looking up from sorting the

different music printouts into folders. Choir practice had let out twenty minutes before, but he had some things to organize.

"So how were things at the kiddie zoo?"

"You're beginning to sound like your wife."

Nate laughed, and Jared glanced up, a grin edging across his features. It had been a difficult practice; "zoo" about defined it, what with Jim-Jim the Peril instigating all manner of pranks, yanking Kitty's ponytail, and getting into more mischief besides. The kid had a voice that should accompany a halo, but sometimes Jared wondered if horns hid beneath his red hair.

"You look like you could use a reprieve," Nate said, taking a seat on the bench. The sanctuary where they practiced every Saturday almost echoed in the afternoon quiet. No more cries of "I'm telling!" giggles, or chattering filled the white-steepled church.

"Brother. And how!" Jared exclaimed, sticking the folders in his briefcase.

"You should come to Jill's this Wednesday. We're following a schematic of New Testament readings the pastor sent different groups, and just between you and me, we could also use another good hand at the pool table afterward."

Jared laughed. He'd shot pool over at Nate and Carly's a few times before. The pool table had been a housewarming-wedding gift to the couple from Nate's father.

"I thought the Bible study at Jill's was mainly for young married couples."

Nate looked at him as if he'd swallowed a minnow. "What gave you that idea?"

"Well, could be because the group is composed of couples, all who've been recently married."

"I didn't start going there until after Carly and I married, but Carly attended before that."

"Oh yeah?" Jared mulled it over. "I might give it a try, then."

"Need directions?"

"No, I've got it covered." Jared picked up his briefcase. "I better scoot. I'm expected at Tom and Carol's for supper."

Nate walked with him through the front doors, and Jared pulled out his keys to lock the church, noticing that it had started to rain again. Outside under the eaves, he saw two children with their backs to the wall.

"I'll catch you later," Nate said with a wave. He took off at a jog for his car.

"Mindy, Kitty, what are you girls still doing here?" Jared asked, holding the door open.

"Mom didn't come," Mindy said.

"She must be running late," Jared assured. "Come inside, out of the rain."

The girls hurried through the door, obviously glad he'd found them.

Sprinkles of water darkened their T-shirts, but they didn't look as if they'd been outside too long. He hoped the rain would pass soon. A streak of lightning followed that thought.

"I'll bet she forgot about us," Kitty said to Mindy. They stood, hugging themselves, their noses pressed to the glass on each side of the door.

"I doubt she forgot you," Jared said, wondering where they'd gotten such ideas.

"She's been acting weird for weeks," Mindy argued. "All spacey, and sometimes I have to say her name a few times before she answers."

"She probably has a lot on her mind." Jared thought about Mindy's words and wondered if Sharon's behavior had to do with Andy. "You two should help her out whenever you can. Do your chores and do what she tells you. Don't give her a hard time." He tempered his words with kindness.

"We don't." Mindy's eyes were wide with sincerity. "Honest."

"How come you stopped coming over?" Kitty wanted to know. "Don't you like us anymore?"

"Sure, I like you. I teach you songs every Saturday, don't I?" Jared felt put on the spot and peered out the window, hoping to glimpse his aunts' coupe.

"But how come you don't come to our house anymore?" Kitty insisted.

Jared paused; he didn't want to say anything that would make it worse for Sharon. "The supper your mom made me was a payback for the trip to the mall. That's all."

"She never paid anyone else back like that," Mindy said.

"What do you mean?"

"Whenever Leslie did us a favor, she never made her food. And she never used her best dishes, except when you came over."

That bit of news intrigued Jared. He had thought his chance with the girls' mom had ended with her announcement that they shouldn't see one another again, even as friends. Now he wondered.

At the sound of a horn honking, the girls spun around to the window. "She's here!" Kitty squealed, and they ran outside. Mindy tore open the passenger door, Kitty the back door, and in that moment, Sharon and Jared made eye contact.

Jared raised his hand in greeting; Sharon paused and then did the same before saying something to the girls, then returning her attention to the rain-spattered windshield, which the wipers worked to keep clear.

Jared watched the car pull away, the tires making wet sounds along the pavement. The girls waved to him, their faces almost pressed against the glass, and Jared smiled.

Maybe, just maybe, he had heard God right after all.

seven

Sharon helped Jill and Leslie prepare the food, setting it on the counter buffet-style. Everyone had brought a dish, and Sharon's french-fried onions over creamy green beans had garnered quite a few approving glances. As she shoved ice into cups and set them along the bar, the doorbell rang.

"A late arrival," Jill murmured. "I wonder who it could be. Hon?"

"I've got it," Ted answered his wife. Sharon heard the sound of the door opening in the next room. "Jared! It's good to see you, buddy. Come in and join the party."

The moment Ted said his name, Sharon dropped the cup. A good thing she'd held it poised over the ice chest and it only hit the cubes. She fetched it out and, with trembling hands, resumed her task.

Jared had come? Had Leslie known he would when she invited Sharon to the Bible study last week?

A glance toward her friend showed Leslie's surprise at seeing Jared walk into the kitchen, where the group had gathered. Sharon felt his presence without needing to look. The sound of his rich voice greeting the others brought chill bumps over her arms that had nothing to do with the frozen air of the chest. She pulled out the cup and carefully set it at the end of the row, next to the other six. Wiping her hands on her jeans, she turned.

Jared seemed just as shocked to see her. His blue jeans and maroon pullover seemed to make the other men fade into the background. Something in his eyes flamed to life as he looked at her, making it difficult for her to swallow.

"Hi, Sharon."

"Jared."

He held her gaze a few seconds longer, then, as if sensing her unease, focused his attention on the men's discussion of the upcoming football season.

Sharon forced herself to concentrate on her task as she filled an extra cup with ice for the new arrival.

After Ted said the blessing over the food, they ate. Sharon took a seat at the table between Leslie and Carly, who told the news about a young friend of hers with excitement. Jared joined the other men in the den, making it easier for Sharon to relax, though knowing he sat only a room away made her tingle with a strange awareness of his presence. His warm voice rose above the other men's as he joked and laughed with them.

"I was floored when Kimmers told me the news," Carly said. "A friend I met on the trail years ago. You might have seen her at church. Pretty, going on nineteen, walks with a white cane?"

Sharon nodded.

"She's been blind for a few years now, and they thought it would be permanent." She looked at Jill. "This new procedure isn't as risky as the ones she could have gotten years ago. She and her dad decided against them, and the doctor told her she's the perfect candidate for this one."

"I think it's amazing," Jill said. "Technology and medicine certainly have advanced in this past year alone."

"When is Kim's surgery?" Leslie asked.

"Nothing has been scheduled yet. I'll let you know when."

"Are she and Chris still going out together?" Jill asked.

"Oh, yeah. He's head over heels in love, has been ever since he was a groomsmen at our wedding and Kim was my bridesmaid. From what she told me, she feels the same about Chris. Chris is Nate's cousin," Carly explained to Sharon. "And Kimmers is already like part of the family. She came with Chris to Nate's family reunion this past summer. Everyone adores her."

"So they're that serious?" Leslie asked. "They're still so young."

"It wouldn't surprise me if they ended up marrying sometime in the future. They're rarely apart."

The women expressed their delight at such an idea.

"I got an announcement card from Sierra and Bart the other day," Jill said. She smiled at Sharon. "Good mates of ours who joined us on the Long Trail and came to our Bible studies. They moved to Phoenix two years ago. Anyway, Sierra had twins! Can you believe it?"

"I know," Carly enthused. "I got a card from Cat, too. I think it's fantastic!"

Sharon smiled at Carly's use of nicknames for her friends. The talk evolved to the children.

"Great news," Jill said. "Ted's niece agreed to come over and babysit on Bible study nights. Not only that, but they'll have their own Bible-incorporated playtime and teachings. She works in the children's church and is full of ideas." She smiled at Sharon. "So be sure to bring your kids next time."

"Thanks, I will. The sisters were thrilled to spend time with them tonight. They're making chocolate chip cookies."

"The sisters. . .you mean Jared's aunts?"

"Yes." Sharon took a quick bite of fruit salad, glad for something on which to focus her attention. "They dote on the kids as if they were their grandchildren."

She didn't miss the pleased looks that Leslie, Carly, and Jill exchanged, but to her relief, no one raised questions about Sharon and Jared or a relationship. If he overheard any speculation like she'd endured at the park, she would have burned with mortification.

Once the women stored the food in the refrigerator, they gathered in the next room for Bible study. Sharon wondered if it was mere coincidence that the only available seat for her was beside Jared on the sofa.

She sank to the cushion beside him, and he gave her a friendly smile.

"How have you been, Sharon?"

"Great." She returned his smile. "Helping the kids get ready to start a new school. Their first day is just around the corner." *The girls miss you, and I don't know what to do about it, since I feel the same but don't want to feel this way.*

"I've seen the girls at choir practice, of course, but how's Andy?"

"As well as can be expected, I guess." Her smile wavered; she tried not to show concern.

His expression gentled. "What's up? Has he been giving you problems?"

From anyone else, Sharon might have taken offense at the inquisitive remark. But she felt relief that Jared had opened the door for her to talk about Andy. She assumed it was because Jared knew about their past. She'd told very few people.

"I worry about him. He's been so distant lately, hardly talks to me anymore, and he spends too much time in his room."

Jared thought a moment. "Have you taken him to see the moose calf?"

"Why, no. . ." Sharon wondered if something so small could have had such a big effect on her son. Remembering his behavior the first few days after they rescued the animal, she realized it must. "I'd completely forgotten I promised the kids we'd visit again; I've been so busy. But then, he didn't bring it up, either," she added in confusion.

"I guess he figures if he did you might ask me to drive you there again."

"And so he picked the most appealing scenario of the two choices—to stay away from the farm," Sharon agreed. "I'm sorry." She winced as she realized how bad that sounded.

Jared shrugged. "It didn't take an anvil to fall on my head for me to figure out Andy doesn't like me."

"Not just you, Jared. I think he'd be that way with any man."

"I know."

Their conversation ended as Jill began the study. Everyone opened their Bibles to 1 Corinthians. With amusement, Sharon noticed that handwritten notes and fluorescent highlights marked the pages of Jared's Bible, as well as her own. The study continued, the reading concluded, and Jill opened the floor for anyone to express what they'd gained from the reading. New to the study, Sharon kept quiet, wishing to observe this first time. Jared had no such compunction. She listened, amazed by his perception, inspired by his fervent and beautiful expressions of what the verses meant to him. She agreed with so many things he said; other remarks of his took her mind along new paths and struck a chord deep within.

After the study concluded, Jill and Leslie grabbed snacks while the others went down to the basement game room. A refrigerator there contained sparkling sodas, and Carly filled orders behind the wet bar, opening liter bottles and pouring sodas into glasses. Sharon helped and handed Jared the fruit spritzer he'd ordered—fruit juices and club soda combined.

"Thanks." His gray-green eyes connected with hers as she handed him his glass.

A rush of warmth she couldn't explain swept over her face. "Sure."

He lifted his glass a few inches as if toasting her before he moved toward a high, round table. He set the glass down and went in search of a cue.

How? How did he do that? Jared possessed the ability to stir something deep inside her without even touching her. He'd made no physical contact with her since his arrival, not even to shake her hand in greeting or share in a hug as he'd done with the others.

"Sharon!"

"What?" She jumped at the shock of Carly's voice near her ear, louder than usual.

"I asked what you wanted to drink." Carly's dark eyes gleamed in amusement as they darted to Jared, then back to Sharon. "But you seem to have your mind on other things at the moment."

"I think I'll have a fruit spritzer, too," Sharon said making a point to ignore Carly's blatant teasing.

"A popular choice tonight." Carly's mouth quirked at the corners.

"I happen to like fruit," Sharon insisted. Both women glanced at one another, then burst out laughing. Sharon couldn't help herself; Carly's gregarious personality might at times set her on edge, but for the most part, her warmth put Sharon completely at ease.

"Well, that's terrific, Angel. Fruit is good for you."

"Angel?"

"My new nickname for you. Besides the fact that you look like one, I happen to know you sing like one, too."

"Not anymore. I don't sing anymore," she elaborated under her breath, hoping Carly would leave it at that.

"Hmm," Carly studied her a moment, then smiled. "Well, I could always call you Fruit-jitters, since you're so jittery and 'happen to like fruit.'"

This brought on another gale of laughter from both of them, and before Carly walked away, she said with a wink, "I think I'll just stick with Angel."

The game commenced—guys against the girls. As she'd warned the other women, Sharon hadn't practiced, and only after a number of turns did she pick up old skills.

"Want a few pointers?" Jared asked from across the table as she practiced in between games.

"Sure." Sharon had relaxed in the past fifteen minutes, joining in the fellowship and laughter, and her earlier uneasiness around him had disappeared. She expected verbal pointers, so when he came around the table to stand behind her, her heart beat a little faster.

Without touching her, he showed her a better way to hold the cue and crouched with her to eye the balls.

"Hey!" Blaine complained, his Texas accent strong. "What're you doin', Jared—goin' on over to the opposition's side? They sure don't need any tips."

"Sh!" Leslie gave her husband a playful swat on his chest, then reached up to whisper something in his ear. Blaine's eyebrows rose as he glanced in Sharon and Jared's direction, and she wondered what Leslie had said.

"The light above casts the ball's shadow onto the table in the direction you want to hit it." Jared's breath warmed her ear. Sharon shivered and closed her eyes for a moment.

"Steady," he said. "Keep your arm steady. Direct your shot as if to hit the shadow, but always keep your focus on the middle of the cue ball. If you hit the edge, it'll miss the mark and could go into a spin. You want to position yourself behind the ball so as to aim for that shadow. You have a good shot for the 2-ball from here. See how the shadow slants toward the corner pocket? Go ahead and try for it."

He stood so close she felt his body warmth, and that made her a bit lightheaded. One fraction of a move on her part, and her back would touch his chest.

"Steady, Sharon," he said. "Now, pull your arm back in one smooth move. Let the stick slide along your fingers, and keep it smooth."

Sharon swallowed and shot, but her arm jerked. She tipped the ball at the bottom, sending it into a jump.

"All right, good try. Let's give it another shot." Jared reached across the table for the white ball and repositioned it. "You need to relax more. You're holding the stick too tight." He paused. "Would you like me to show you what I mean?"

At her bare nod, he moved behind her again. This time, his large hand covered hers, unclamping her stiff fingers and positioning them until they loosely cupped the area near the bottom of the stick. With his other hand, he positioned her hand so that it formed a loose O near the top of the stick. He leaned into her, keeping his warm hands on hers, and pulled the stick back and forth in two graceful moves, the second much more swift. With a loud smack, the cue ball hit the red ball, which zipped toward the corner pocket and plummeted downward.

Sharon caught her breath the moment he touched her, stunned by the sudden awareness that she wanted this. She wanted Jared near. Even more shocking, she wanted him to turn her around and gather her into his arms.

The unexpected image of herself in Jared's embrace made her tense against him; he released her hands, stepping quickly back.

She straightened and licked her bottom lip before she looked up at him. He lifted his gaze from her mouth to her eyes.

"Anyway," he said at last, his voice a bit strained. "That's how it's done."

"Thank you for showing me," she whispered.

A clatter of footsteps on the stairs saved them from further conversation, as those who'd gone upstairs returned, and the second game began. Throughout the game, Sharon felt Jared's eyes on her a few times, but when she looked his way, he averted his gaze.

When his attention focused elsewhere she watched him,

admiring his attractive face and form. His features were strong and masculine but kind; she couldn't remember once seeing his face twisted in an enraged scowl, though he'd had good reason to be angry with her and her kids plenty of times. His body was lithe, trim, strong; she could see the muscles of his back and shoulders ripple beneath his pullover each time he bent low to take a shot. But protectiveness grounded his strength. She knew he would never hit a woman.

She wished now she hadn't told him they couldn't be friends. Twice before the party broke up, she almost told him so, almost asked his forgiveness, almost asked if he would try again. Both times she chickened out, and when everyone said good-bye for the night and went their separate ways, Sharon nursed a heavy heart.

&

"Jared, yoo-hoo, Jared!"

Jared turned outside the church steps to meet his aunts. They each gave him a hug, and he noticed they seemed to bristle with excitement. Their blue eyes sparkled.

"We wanted to invite you over—" Loretta said.

"For Sunday dinner," Josephine finished.

"We've cooked all your favorites."

Josephine nodded. "Roast beef and potatoes with cooked carrots—"

"And creamed corn," Loretta ended.

"Pumpkin pie. . ."

"And pecan, too."

Jared laughed, spreading his hands out as a sign for them to stop. "All right, already, you've convinced me. But as wonderful cooks as you both are, did you really think I'd need that much persuasion?"

"Oh, you are such a charmer," Loretta said.

"A real sweetheart," Josephine added.

Jared smiled. "Only telling it like it is. What time should I come over?"

The sisters looked at one another, then at Jared.

"Why, right now of course," they said in unison.

He chuckled. "I just need to talk to the pastor about the Christmas program, and I'll be there."

"There's still almost three months to go, isn't there?" Loretta asked.

"You must be excited," Josephine added.

Excited wasn't the word. Everything that could fall apart so far had, and Jared didn't want to fail in his first attempt as a choir director. Because many families went out of town at Christmas, the church held the program the week before the holiday, and he found himself wishing for that extra week. One of his leads and three others had recently come down with chicken pox; even though it was too early to worry about a lack in his cast, he knew winter often brought an outbreak of all manner of viruses. Sharon hadn't been at the Bible studies at Jill's for the past four weeks, and Leslie told him that one by one her children had succumbed to another bug going around. Today, he'd seen her and her family across the aisle in the back pew and had given thanks that everyone was well, but he couldn't rid himself of the feeling that something would go wrong with the program.

Once the service ended, he had headed toward Sharon to say hi, but another church member approached her, and he'd backed off.

He missed her. This past month had been harder than he'd expected. At Ted and Jill's, as he'd given Sharon pool tips, when he'd leaned against her, so close he could smell her flowery perfume, his pulse rate had increased and he'd wondered if she could hear his heart beating. It had taken a great deal of self-control not to pull her into his arms and kiss her. He wondered what she would have done if he had. Of course, with the others looking on, giving them no privacy, it hadn't been an option.

After discussing set and performance issues with Pastor Neil, Jared drove to his aunts'. Kitty answered his knock.

"Jared!" She threw her arms around his hips and hugged him hard, burying her cheek in his stomach. "You came back."

Staggered by the unexpected welcome as well as by the identity of the welcoming party, Jared felt tongue-tied.

"Jared!" Mindy rounded the corner of the foyer. "Neatness! Are you eating with us?"

Us?

"Come in, Jared, come in," Loretta said, walking behind Mindy.

Jared had little choice even had he wanted to hold back. Kitty grabbed his hand and dragged him inside, as if impatient with his sluggishness.

"What perfect timing. Dinner's ready," Josephine said, coming behind Loretta.

"You didn't tell me you had other company," he said under his breath to his aunts.

"Oh, Sharon?" Loretta asked.

"She and her family always eat with us on Sundays," Josephine added. "Now come along before the food gets cold."

Having received nothing but welcomes, Jared prepared himself for Sharon's reaction. As he entered the dining room, she turned from setting the table.

She smiled a welcome, her eyes reflecting her delight as though she'd expected him. The afternoon sun highlighted her pale blond hair with golden-white highlights and reminded him of an angel. She wore a simple blue dress with no frills or decorations. It made her eyes even bluer.

"Hi."

For a moment Jared could only stare. This was the first time he'd been this close to her since the Bible study more than a month ago.

"Hi."

A string of questions from Kitty and Mindy forestalled anything else they might have wanted to say to each other.

Dinner progressed much like the first time he'd eaten there with Sharon and her family. Kitty and Mindy asked for more stories from Jared's boyhood, and his aunts embarrassed him by bringing up more of his immature pranks, which he then had to explain and expound upon. Andy glowered at him, wolfed down his food, and ran outside. The aunts fed off one another's sentences and continued to spur everyone on to other topics.

Once the meal concluded, Sharon began removing the dishes from the table, taking them to the kitchen in what he assumed had become her regular after-dinner chore. After she cleared the table of everything but Jared's setting, Loretta and Josephine smiled at him, and Josephine tilted her head toward the kitchen in a blatant sign that he should join their other guest.

"I think I'll take a breather on the porch while the weather's still nice," Loretta said. "Sister, won't you join me?"

"Why I'd be delighted to, sister."

Jared rolled his eyes at their obvious ploy and grinned. "If you two were any clearer, they'd have to mark your foreheads with masking tape so no one walks into you," he joked.

Josephine tittered as she followed Loretta outside.

Jared finished the last bites of his meal, picked up his empty plate and glass, and carried them to the kitchen. Sharon filled one side of the sink with sudsy water, the other with clear rinse water. His aunts didn't use their automatic dishwasher, claiming it left ugly spots, and weren't willing to try newer models with the no-spot guarantee. So the dishwasher's sole purpose had become the drying rack.

He set his plate on the countertop and moved next to Sharon. She glanced at him, smiled, and continued her task. From the open window over the sink, a mild breeze wafted inside the room, which felt hot and stifling from dinner preparations and the cleanup involved.

"I hope you don't mind if I come in and pester you," Jared joked.

"Pester me? Are you kidding? It will be nice to hold a conversation with another adult for a change. I'm just about burned out on the topic of cartoon characters, comic book heroes, and the back-to-school blues the girls have been singing."

She swiped a plate clean with a sudsy rag and let it sink into the clear rinse water without letting her hand touch it. Though more steam rose from its surface than the side Sharon worked out of, Jared stuck his hand down to grab the plate. He winced as the liquid scalded, and snapped the plate up and to the bottom dishwasher rack in one swift, circuslike move, almost losing his grip.

"Maybe you'd better wait until the water cools," Sharon suggested with a half-concerned, half-amused smile. "Or your aunts might be minus a few dishes."

She had a point.

He cradled his hand beneath his armpit.

"Are you okay?" she asked.

"Never better."

Not sure of what to do with himself, but wanting to remain in her company, he moved behind Sharon to the opposite counter that angled with the countertop where she stood, making an L shape. He shook his hand a few times but saw no burns of any degree, though the skin had reddened. His back to the counter, he braced his hands against the Formica and hoisted himself to sit on top.

Sharon turned her head to look at him, her eyebrows lifted.

"What?" Jared spread his hands wide.

With a little smile of disbelief, she shook her head and plucked another dish out of the soapy water. "Nothing."

He watched for a while admiring the outline of her face.

"Do you really do all those pranks they said you did?"

He gave a sheepish grin. "Yeah, and worse."

"Worse?"

"Taping the kitchen sprayer's lever down so that when my sister turned on the water, she would get it—full in the face."

Sharon chuckled. "Now that was bad."

"You haven't heard the worst part yet," Jared said with a pained smile. "My mom was the one who turned on the water, not Amy. Amy got sick, so Mom took over Amy's chore of washing the dishes that night."

Sharon laughed. "Your poor mom."

"I like it when you do that," Jared said his tone soft.

"Do what?" Puzzled, she glanced at him.

"Laugh. It's good on you. You should do it more often."

Her face was already rosy from standing over a steaming sink, but with the way she looked down, he felt she might be blushing. Knowing he'd embarrassed her without meaning to, Jared slid down from the counter and returned to the rinse water. Skimming his fingertips over the top, he realized the temperature had cooled enough for him to pull out the clean dishes. He cleared the sink, setting the tableware in the dishwasher racks to dry.

"You know," she said after a minute, "this old-fashioned way of doing this is nice when it's shared. More, I don't know— homey? Instead of just quickly done and over with. It takes longer, but it gives people a chance to talk."

"My family is very old-fashioned when it comes to. . .well,

just about everything," Jared admitted. "Though on the farm we've made some modern adjustments for convenience' sake."

Sharon spent an inordinate length of time cleaning out a glass, and Jared realized she had something on her mind.

"Kitty and Mindy really want to see your maple sugar farm next spring," she said after a moment as she handed the glass to him.

He rinsed it. "The invitation is always open. We get tourists year round, and my family would love to meet you. I've told them a lot about you." He cut off his words, wondering if he'd said too much.

She cast him a sideways glance along with another smile, this one self-conscious.

"When we talked before the Bible study at Jill's, I said some things. . . ." Her words trailed off, and he kept himself from urging her to continue, patience never a great asset of his. "Truth is," she said as she washed another plate, "maybe I was wrong."

"Wrong?" He tried to follow her.

She quit rubbing the washrag in repetitive circles and looked at him straight on. "About us being friends. If the offer still stands, I'd like to take you up on it again."

Jared felt a twinge of disappointment. She only mentioned friendship, nothing more personal. But he realized a friendship with him was a major step for her. And he'd always known he would need to take things slow.

"Of course the offer still stands. I'm glad you changed your mind." He wondered if he should take it a step further, and decided honesty was always best. "I've missed you."

"I've missed you, too," she whispered, peering shyly up at him.

"Well then. . ." He wanted to suggest another outing but refrained and let his words trail off. He should let her take the lead since she'd opened up negotiations between them again.

"Well then." She smiled and pulled her lower lip in her mouth in contemplation. "I'm taking the kids to Hugh's farm this coming Saturday; he's about to release the moose calf to the wild, and I promised Andy he could say good-bye. Would you like to come with us? Afterward maybe we could grab a bite to eat at a restaurant the kids enjoy."

She expected him to wait a whole week? Jared corralled his impatience to see her before then. Until that moment, he hadn't thought he'd spend time with her again at all.

"That would be great," he said. "I look forward to it."

eight

Mindy opened the door to Jared's knock.

"Hi, Jared. Mom's not home yet. She called and said she's running late, and to just come in and make yourself at home."

"Thanks." He smiled at the girl as he stepped inside. "Have you been practicing your lines for the program?"

"Yeah, but I gotta get back to my homework now before we go to your aunts' to be babysat. Mom said I have to finish before then."

Before he could say another word, Mindy ran to her room. Her door slammed, and Jared exhaled a long breath, looking around the empty den. Since their second trip to see the moose a month and a half before, Jared had taken Sharon and the kids out twice, to the movies and to eat at a kid-oriented restaurant. Tonight was the first night he would be with Sharon alone. Not a date, he reminded himself. You couldn't call Christmas shopping a date, and Sharon had shown no interest in crossing the sole-friendship sector. No matter, tonight would be the first occasion he and Sharon would spend time with one another, without the children, without his aunts, just the two of them alone. He wondered why he should feel so nervous.

Jared shed his jacket on the ottoman and walked into the kitchen as he'd done three Saturdays ago when he'd asked for a glass of water. Whenever he came here, he'd asked for water, due in part to the dry mouth he got each time he saw Sharon, who seemed more beautiful every time he saw her. Sharon had been busy the last time and had told him to help himself. He didn't think she'd mind him repeating the act, since she'd conveyed through Mindy the message to make himself at home.

He pulled a glass from the cupboard and turned on the faucet. A stream of ice-cold water hit him full in the face. Dropping the glass in the sink, he brought his hands up to shield himself from the watery assault. With one hand he groped for the faucet lever and turned the tap off. He grabbed the hand towel from where it hung and wiped water from his eyes.

A quick study of the sprayer showed duct tape held down the lever and a clamp that looked like it came from a children's toy set had been rigged into position straight towards Jared's face.

Andy's snicker heralded his entrance into the kitchen. "Did you have an accident, Mr. Crisp?"

Before Jared could answer, he heard Kitty squeal in glee and her running footsteps from down the hall. "Jared's here!" She turned the corner into the kitchen and stopped in her tracks, her eyes going wide.

With his hair dripping into his wet face and his blue shirt plastered to his shoulders, he knew he must look a sight.

The sound of the front door opening and closing made them all turn toward the doorway. Within moments, Sharon entered. Her mouth dropped open.

"Jared! What happened?"

Jared glanced at Andy, saw the bitter challenge in his eyes, and resumed toweling dry. "I had an accident."

"An accident?"

"Yeah, an accident."

Andy broke away from Jared's stare, looking uncomfortable.

Jared smiled at Sharon. "Are you ready to go?"

"I just have to get out of these work clothes and into some jeans. I'll be right with you." She cast a curious glance between Andy and Jared but left without another word. Kitty followed her.

Jared rubbed at the dampness on his shirt. Without looking at Andy, he spoke. "I take it you were eavesdropping on us while your mother and I did the dishes at my aunts' house several weeks ago."

"What do you mean?" The boy's words were wary. "I didn't do nothin'."

"The window was open, we were talking, and you'd gone outside. It doesn't take a mathematician to put the pieces together, Andy." He pulled the tape from the sprayer and held it up.

Andy narrowed his eyes, lifting his chin.

"This doesn't look like something either Mindy or Kitty would do." Jared undid the clamp that kept the sprayer nozzle aimed high. "And this, unless I miss my guess, is from a sci-fi toy set of a popular movie. My nephew Billy has one like it."

Surprise lit the boy's eyes a moment before the usual cynicism took over. "So if you knew I did it, why didn't you tell Mom?"

"Because this is just between you and me. I don't want to get your mother involved. She has enough worries right now."

The boy crossed his arms and scowled at Jared. "Yeah, well maybe you should just leave, and she wouldn't have any more worries."

"Have I done something to hurt you, Andy?"

"What do you mean?"

"Have I done anything to make you dislike me? I helped you save the moose calf, I took you to see it; I try to help you guys out whenever I can."

"Yeah, well, we don't need your help! So you can just stop helping us to make me like you because I'll never like you."

Jared laid the towel on the countertop and placed his palms against the edge, leaning his weight on them. "Let's get something straight. I'm not helping you for any reason other than I want to. Life is a whole lot nicer when there's not so much hate involved, Andy. Did you know it's easier to smile than it is to frown? The muscles work harder when you frown."

Disregarding his words, Andy's scowl grew even blacker. "You're not my father!"

"I didn't say I was."

"Yeah, well, don't try to be. Because you'll never be my father!" Andy raced from the room, and soon a door slammed down the hallway.

Jared sighed, wondering if he would ever make peace with the boy. Sweeping his hands through his damp hair, he tried to bring it to order. He had to chuckle. He supposed it was fitting that after years of instigating childhood pranks he should get his own dose. The Bible did say that you reap what you sow.

The sprayer safely disengaged, Jared pulled the glass from the sink, glad to see it hadn't chipped or cracked. He filled the glass with water and drank down half. Sharon appeared in the doorway, now in a cozy-looking gray fleece shirt and blue jeans, and Jared set down the glass.

"You look great." And she did. No matter what she wore, she made the outfit. Her choices always brought out the sheen of her hair, the startling blue of her eyes, and flattered her slender figure.

She smiled but seemed uncertain.

"Is everything okay?" he asked.

"I don't know, is it?" She moved toward him, her eyes taking in the strip of duct tape and the clamp at a glance. She raised her eyebrows as she looked at him. "An accident?"

"Yeah. I should've never turned on the water."

"Funny, Jared." She didn't look amused. "You shouldn't shield him like that. He doesn't need to think he can get away with this kind of behavior."

"I didn't want to upset you."

"I'm his mother."

"I know. But we talked, and I handled it." Jared winced when he thought of what a mess he'd made of things. "As a former prankster, I recognized that's all this was."

"Was it?" She shook her head. "I'm not so sure. But let's get one thing straight right now—no more deception. Even little white lies."

"You're right, and I'm sorry. I wasn't thinking."

"I know. You were just trying to get him off the hook." She sighed. "I'm not sure we should do this tonight. It's a good sale, but there'll probably be another. Maybe I should call your aunts and cancel; I'd hate for him to pull another of his stunts."

"I wouldn't worry about it; he'll behave for them. And my aunts love spending time with your kids. They told me so. Loretta doesn't have grandchildren, and they both dote on your kids. Besides. . ." He grinned. "They rented the new Oliver Twist movie. I'm sure they would be disappointed if they couldn't watch it with the kids."

"Well, a good dose of Oliver may be just what Andy needs," she mused. "It might help him be thankful for what he has and stop pouting about what he doesn't have."

Jared nodded, pleased that in the past few weeks she'd grown comfortable enough with him to discuss personal issues, at times asking for his viewpoint.

"All right," Sharon agreed. "Let's do this."

≈

Once they dropped off the children at his aunts' house, Jared drove Sharon to the same mall they'd visited months earlier. Sharon noted the outside Christmas decorations though Thanksgiving was still a week away. Inside, holly and tinsel decked the stores, and piped Christmas music from an earlier decade played over hidden speakers.

"Leslie told me the toy store is located near this department store, but I guess we should find a directory."

"I guess." Jared shoved his fists into his jacket, nervous, as if he feared another experience like last time, and she chuckled at the memory of Kitty her clothes diva.

Outside the department store, they located a guide. Sharon found the toy store in the green grid, and noted it was twelve stores down. Quite a walk, but she'd worn athletic shoes, having expected the exercise. She noticed Jared glance with interest into each store's front window, as if he'd never seen the items on display before.

"Anytime you want to stop and look, let me know," Sharon said. "I know you need to do your Christmas shopping, too."

"Well, no. I don't shop."

"You don't shop?" She gave him a curious, sidelong glance.

"Boxes of Crisp's maple fudge and other maple sugar products from our line to my friends. Gift certificates that I buy online for the family." He shook his head. "I'm not really into store shopping."

Sharon stopped walking and turned to stare at him. "Then why. . . ?"

"Why what?" His brow lifted in question.

"Why did you say you wanted to go Christmas shopping with me when I brought it up the other day?"

He grinned and grasped her elbow to steer her back into a walk. "Let's head for that toy store, shall we? Before those sale items are gone."

Sharon allowed him to steer her, noticing he moved his hand from her arm to the small of her back as they walked through the crowd. What surprised her wasn't that he touched her but that she welcomed his touch. Yet she feared that allowing such actions now could only cause problems in the future.

With relief and regret, she felt him drop his hand away as they entered the toy store.

The front display featured a huge, tabletop electronic building game encased in plastic, set up for shoppers to test. Jared's attention riveted to the beeping rubber-and-steel construction machine that a young boy worked hard to manage, using the lever on a control box to manipulate a steel claw.

Sharon's mouth twitched when she saw the light of boyish interest sparkle in Jared's eyes. "Go ahead and watch. It shouldn't take me long."

Without waiting for his answer, she picked up a shopping basket and studied the aisles, easily locating the doll section. She pulled a clipping of the sale ad from her purse and surveyed shelves with the help of the photograph. Soon she found its match. Three left, and two boxes dented, the film of plastic broken. She was glad now she hadn't put off the shopping trip another day.

All year, she put a little into savings each paycheck to make sure her children would have a Christmas. She would never forget the Christmas when she was married to Mark and the kids had woken up to nothing. She had planned to go shopping Christmas Eve but had discovered Mark had disappeared on one of his weeklong jaunts, taking the money with him. She had dipped her hand into the jar, which should have been filled with bills from the tips she'd earned at work, and found only pennies, nickels, and dimes. Mark had even taken the quarters.

A kind neighbor, Mrs. McGraff, learned of the incident when she saw Mindy sitting on the porch, crying that Santa had forgotten her. Thirty minutes later, the elderly woman appeared at the front door with boxes of hard candy and a batch of homemade cookies for the children to enjoy. Also in her arms had been a stuffed toy lion, used but still in good condition, a drawing set, and some unused coloring books and crayons. She explained to the children that Santa must have left them on her doorstep by mistake and that she'd heard the reindeer's harness and had peeked out of her window for a "look-see."

Mindy, then three, stared with huge eyes at the gray-haired woman, but Sharon would always remember the smile on her daughter's face as she grabbed the stuffed lion and hugged it to her heart. Mrs. McGraff later explained to Sharon that she kept toys for when her grandkids visited and hoped Sharon didn't mind them being used. Sharon, unable to talk at first for the happy tears, had squeezed the woman's hands in gratitude, calling her a Christmas angel.

Now that Sharon was a Christian, she wondered if God had sent Mrs. McGraff to them and had been looking out for Sharon and her kids even before she'd learned of His existence. As many times as she could have died from Mark's outbursts of anger, as many times as she and the children escaped, miraculously running into others who'd helped them, Sharon knew God must have been watching over her family from the start. At the women's shelter, Leslie had once told Sharon someone must have been praying hard for her. Remembering her grandfather in Ohio—whom the family had rejected upon his Christian conversion—Sharon wondered if he prayed for them.

She went down another aisle and located a football for Andy, hoping to steer his interest in sports and provide an acceptable outlet for his anger. A children's confectionery-bakery set for Mindy seemed a good choice. Since watching the flying-car fantasy movie and hearing about Jared's occupation, Mindy's interests revolved around joining a candy-making factory the first chance one opened in Goosebury. Adding several small, inexpensive toys for stocking stuffers to the basket, Sharon completed her task. For Jared's aunts, her friends, and the kids' teachers, she planned to make homemade batches of cookies or fudge, a tradition she'd started with the children two years ago and one Mindy would be even more enthused about this year.

Unable to fit the bulky bakery-set box into the basket, she wrapped her arm around the carton, holding it to her side. She walked to the front and stopped at the end of the aisle, astounded at the sight that met her eyes.

The boy who'd operated the electronic gizmo had gone; Jared now sat on the stool, his tall, trim form leaning forward, with the soles of his shoes on the rungs and his knees pressed against the table. His long fingers wiggled the lever of the hand-control box as he manipulated the steel claw to pick up a toy log. A lock of dark hair, usually swept back from his forehead, dangled across his brow. The tip of his tongue touched his top lip in a picture of studied concentration, and Sharon stood still as she watched him without his being aware.

A smile spread across her face. Jared was unlike any man she'd ever known; from the moment of their bizarre meeting, he had stunned her, confused her, and intrigued her. Her initial anxiety in his presence disappeared within twenty-four hours of knowing him, and now she saw another side to him she'd never realized existed. The heart of the little boy still lived inside the man.

"Excuse me," a woman said behind her.

Sharon apologized for blocking the aisle and moved aside. She would have loved to watch him longer and didn't want to disrupt his fun, but he caught sight of her, so she moved toward him.

"I always thought of going into construction." With a semi-bashful smile, he set down the control.

"Was this before or after you became an employee at your family's maple-sugar farm?"

"Well, I do run pipelines between trees and clear fallen branches from the paths," he said in mock defense. "That could be considered construction."

"It's certainly constructive," she laughed.

He noticed the box under her arm for the first time and stood. "Let me take that. Too bad this store doesn't have carts."

Unaccustomed to receiving help from a man, she felt a bit strange letting him take the huge box from her. It wasn't heavy, but it was awkward. "Thanks. My arm feels as if it's going numb."

"How long have you been holding this?" He easily hefted it beneath his arm, carrying it on his hip. "You should have asked for my help earlier."

"I didn't want to bother you."

"Bother me?" He seemed confused. "Sharon, I'm here for you. If you need my help, ask."

"I'm just not used to that sort of thing, Jared, asking for help or expecting it. My stepfather wasn't well-bred, and Mark certainly wasn't; I doubt either of them knew any manners at all. They expected their women to wait on them and be their slaves—the cavemen of the twenty-first century," she joked.

"Well, I'm not like them," he said, his expression serious.

"No, you're not. But then, I'm not your woman," she said before she thought.

The words hung between them, and she wished she could retrieve the tactless remark, even though it was true.

"No, you're not," he agreed quietly. "But I'm no Neanderthal, either. A woman like you deserves to be treated like a lady."

Uneasy with the personal direction his remarks had taken, she lifted her basket a fraction. "I should pay for these." He nodded.

Once they left the toy store, they remained quiet, and she hoped she hadn't offended him. Catching sight of one of her favorite kinds of stores, she grabbed his arm to stop him. He looked at her in surprise.

"Have you ever been to a Dollar Store?" she asked.

"Uh, nope, can't say that I have," he said.

"Well, you're in for a treat. Come on."

He answered her smile with a lopsided grin. Thankful the ice had again thawed between them, she led him through the crowded store, crammed with numerous baskets and bins of assorted merchandise. They maneuvered the aisles like little children let loose in a candy store. Jared slipped a reindeer puppet over his hand and made it talk to her in a high squeaky voice and "kiss" her nose. Sharon giggled both at his antics and at the anxious expression of the woman shopper who approached the aisle, studying Jared as if he belonged in a straitjacket.

Sharon couldn't remember ever having such fun with a guy. She held up cheap, dangly earrings to her ears for his advice, and he shook his head at each one, which she then replaced with another. His smile grew wide at a pair of long tasseled rhinestones. "Perfect," he grinned, then insisted on buying her a rhinestone tiara to go with them, placing the silver crown on her head and calling her "princess." She didn't even object to wearing it through the mall, despite the odd looks she received from other shoppers. Jared's fun-loving nature was contagious.

At the glass door leading out of the mall, he opened it for her and swept low in a bow. He straightened once she swept past and nodded his head in greeting at two elderly ladies who tittered behind their gloves as he kept the door open for them.

"Young love," Sharon heard one of them say to the other as the two women walked away. "So crazy, so sweet."

Sharon knew Jared must have heard, though thankfully he didn't bring up the woman's comment.

At his aunts' house, they rounded up the kids, and he drove them home.

"What's that on your head, Mama?" Kitty wanted to know.

"Hmm? Oh, just a crown," she said as if it was an everyday occurrence for her to wear a piece of jewelry from a children's play set.

In the rearview mirror, she saw the girls shrug at one another, though Andy looked less than pleased. Once Jared pulled his car into her drive, he cut the ignition and got out, going around to her side. To her shock, Andy bolted out of the backseat and opened her door before Jared could get there.

"Thanks, sweetie," she said, peering at him, curious.

The girls ran into the house, but Andy seemed intent on loitering. Sharon gave him a pointed look, but he pretended not to understand.

"Andy, it's bedtime," she reminded.

"Aren't you coming, too, Mom?" he asked, sending a baleful look Jared's way.

"In a minute. Go on."

With a scowl that had become common for him, he took off for the house.

"I had fun tonight," Sharon said when she and Jared were alone.

"So did I. I didn't know shopping could be that much fun."

Only with you. She had always considered it a chore before.

He came close to her, so close she saw the moon's reflection in his incredible eyes, making them shine almost silver. For one breathless moment, she felt sure he would kiss her. Her heartbeats escalated as she stood motionless. Her gaze dropped to his slightly parted mouth, which lowered a fraction toward hers.

The inhuman *yowwwwl* of a cat made them both jump away, and Jared's chuckle sounded self-conscious. Taking her hand in his, he bowed low over it, as if addressing royalty. His soft lips brushed her knuckles, and this time her heart jumped at the tingles that remained when he straightened.

"Good night, fair princess. The time has arrived that I must ride off into the black evening on yon charger, as daybreak shall, in due course, commence." At her raised brows, he added, "Mrs. Beldon's literature class—Shakespeare, sophomore year."

Sharon laughed as she waved him off. "You nut. Off with you. Find some other lady to beleaguer with your questionable charms." She remembered a bit of Shakespeare from high school, too.

He clasped his hands over his heart in a dramatic pose. "Oh, the arrows of disdain doth pierce through my heart. Have you not a drop of mercy, dear lady?"

"None. Motherhood sucked it all out of me." She grinned. "Begone with you then."

"Alas and alack, I fear my words are of little merit here." He winked. "And so I shall make my fondest farewells."

"Isn't that what you've been doing for the past five minutes?"

He laughed at her quick comeback, saluting her with a more modern, pilot-type gesture, two fingers away from his brow. "G'night, Sharon."

"G'night, Jared."

She was still smiling as his car pulled out of the drive, and he stuck his hand out the window in a wave, one she returned.

The silence that settled in around her once his car disappeared down the lane seemed lonelier than ever. And in that moment before she turned to enter the house, she realized she hadn't wanted him to go.

"Jared, what are you doing to me?" she whispered.

A movement at Andy's bedroom window caught her attention. Her son's face stared out at her, his expression in shadow, and she frowned when she realized he'd been spying.

nine

At the Crisp farm, the onset of the holidays meant a huge boost in workload, with hundreds of orders for Christmas gifts readied and shipped to customers. The advance of autumn always brought more tourists to the farm, as well. But on the actual holidays, the family took time to rest and enjoy each other's company.

After Thanksgiving dinner, the men congregated around the TV to watch football, while the women clustered in the kitchen to talk while they cleaned.

Jared tried to get interested in the game. Normally, he liked football, but today he had too much on his mind. At halftime, he slipped on his coat and wandered outdoors onto the porch, studying the view.

Forests of snow-flocked sugar maples hemmed in all sides of the farmhouse, and in the background, he saw the rooftops of the buildings they used to make the maple syrup and store it, as well as that of a small gift shop. A thick blanket of snow covered the ground, and Jared wondered what Sharon would do if he drove up in a horse-drawn sleigh. She might enjoy the experience a lot more than the first time she'd ridden behind Tamany.

After their Christmas-shopping excursion, he'd almost kissed her. If the neighborhood cat hadn't picked that moment to start a screeching operetta, he would have. But in hindsight, friends didn't kiss friends, and he worried that if he tried again he might scare her away. He knew she was the one God had chosen for him, but she hadn't experienced that epiphany yet; until and unless she did, they must remain just friends. His mouth twitched at a bumper sticker he'd once read—"God, I need patience—now!" Still, in retrospect, he couldn't call a wait of over ten years impatient.

The door opened behind him. "Jared?"

His mom walked up to him, wearing her pink pullover sweater, her arms crossed over her chest.

"You shouldn't be out here without a coat, Mom," Jared quietly scolded.

She chuckled. "Are you kidding? It's nice to leave that hot, steamy kitchen." Her green eyes, almost lost between her laugh creases, studied him. They weren't laughing now. "Are you all right, son?"

"Sure. Never better."

"Didn't you like dessert?"

"What a thing for one of the best cooks in Goosebury to ask." He laughed. "With a wall of blue ribbons to prove it." He pulled her up against him in a one-armed hug.

"In jams only. But you didn't ask for seconds of pumpkin pie. And you always ask for seconds."

"Maybe I'm trying to watch my weight?"

She slapped his stomach hard.

"Ow!" he joked.

"Tight and flat as an ironing board. You're not Tom. Your brother, now he does need to shed a few pounds."

"He must like Carol's cooking." Jared winked as he mentioned Tom's wife.

"Hmph." She studied him closely. "Mrs. Moorehead's niece has come to Vermont to visit over the holidays. She's staying through Christmas."

"That's nice. I'm sure Mrs. Moorehead will love her company since she doesn't get out much," Jared replied, ignoring his mother's obvious insinuation.

"I could introduce the two of you."

"I met Mrs. Moorehead back in fifth grade when she flunked me in spelling."

His mom struck him again.

"Ouch." He laughed. "Hey—now that did hurt."

"So tell me, would it hurt anything for you to go out with her niece one time? She's a nice Christian girl. I met her, and she's very sweet. I know you're waiting for the right woman to come along, but honestly, did God tell you that your mom couldn't give a little nudge?"

"Yes, it would hurt things, and no, He didn't. But I might as well tell you." He paused, wondering how much to reveal. "I found her."

"What?" His mom's eyes grew wide. "Who? What's her name? Does she live here in Goosebury? You cruel, heartless son—why don't you tell your poor mother these things?"

He laughed at her spiel of questions and raised his hand as if to calm a wild filly. "Whoa, easy there. Calm down, Mom. Nothing's set yet, but I'm sure she's the one."

"Well, hallelujah, I never thought I'd see the day. Does this blessed wonder have a name?"

"Sharon Lester."

"The woman with three kids, who works at Loretta and Josephine's shop?"

"That would be the one."

She tilted her head, watching him, as if considering something. "Why didn't you bring her over for Thanksgiving dinner?"

"I invited her, but she'd made other plans."

"Hmm. So when *do* you bring her home to meet the family?"

"I'm working on it. I'm still figuring out a way to broach the subject of a more personal relationship; she's going to take some careful handling."

"What's wrong with her?"

"Wrong with her?" He drew his brows inward, confused.

"That she doesn't see what a treasure you are."

He grinned. "And you wouldn't be just the least bit biased, would you?"

"Not a bit." Her words came sincere. "Just ask the rest of the single women in Goosebury who have, at one time or another, tried to capture your heart. Even your own sister-in-law, before you introduced her to Josh."

Jared chuckled dryly. "Yeah, well, this time I'm the one trying to capture Sharon's heart. I have to go slow; she's been through a lot, especially in her marriage. She's a widow by the way; I wouldn't even think of pursuing a married woman."

"As if I thought you would," she scoffed. "Your character would blind someone if the sun struck it; it's plated in 24 karat."

"Thanks, Mom, but I have my flaws. Remember all the practical jokes? Now and then, I still like to pull a few on my brothers."

Her eyes narrowed. "I'd forgotten about those. Hmm, maybe brass-plated."

"And I had to go and remind you," he said with a mock groan. "I promise you'll meet Sharon soon. Her kids want to see how the maple-sugar farm is run, so I'm going to use that as a lure during the sugaring season, scoundrel that I am."

A smile of wonder tilted his mom's mouth. "You love her."

"Yeah," he admitted for the first time aloud. "I do."

&

"I hate this stuff." Mindy frowned, her head buried against one hand, her elbow propped on the table. She poked at the mound of mashed potatoes and lifted her fork, letting what was on the tines plop to join the rest of the white mass.

"You loved mashed potatoes a week ago," Sharon said with fast dissolving patience. She had worked hard to prepare this

Thanksgiving meal, even making from scratch the potatoes Mindy criticized.

"Why couldn't we have gone to Jared's?" her daughter plaintively shot back.

Kitty also looked up, her expression lackluster. "Did Jared ask us over?"

Mindy had overheard the conversation when Jared invited Sharon last week; Kitty had been in another room.

Andy grabbed his fourth roll, his appetite not the least bit affected. "We don't need to go anywhere else," he said to his sister. "We're a family, right? Just Mom and us, like it's always been. We don't need anyone else."

Just Mom and us. Sharon sighed. "Always" to a child could mean a matter of a few years, which was all it had been. In truth, she hadn't wanted to refuse Jared's invitation to spend Thanksgiving with him and his family. But lately, she'd felt confused by her feelings while in his company. The confusion made her wish to retreat, but when she did, she found all she wanted was to be with him. A vicious cycle she couldn't satisfy. Neither way made her completely happy.

"Why's the turkey all dry?" Mindy complained.

Sharon shoved the gravy bowl her way. "Put some of this on it."

"I don't like gravy. It has black dots floating in it."

"That's pepper."

"I don't like pepper."

Sharon had just about had enough of Mindy's dislikes. She rose from the table and carried dishes to the sink. "Fine, you don't have to eat. And you don't have to eat any cake, either."

"Cake?" Mindy perked up. "What kind of cake?"

"Carrot cake with cream-cheese frosting." Sharon smiled, glad to see she'd interested her cranky daughter at last. "I bought it at the bakery."

"Carrots in cake?" Kitty asked. "Yuk."

"What dork put cheese in icing?" Mindy agreed. "And whoever heard of carrot cake for Thanksgiving?"

Sharon threw down the trash she'd just gathered onto the bar. "Well, that suits me just fine! You don't have to eat any carrot cake." Tears rushed to her eyes, and the children stared at her, agape. "I'll eat the whole cruddy thing myself!"

They didn't respond, and Sharon, humiliated that she'd had a brief emotional meltdown in front of the kids, ran to her room and slammed the door.

She threw herself on her bed, knowing she had acted as much like a child as her kids. She felt horrible for sinking to their level, but she couldn't help herself right now. She felt empty, her heart so heavy it actually hurt to breathe. She did this for them. Couldn't they see that? If she and Jared did grow closer, when it ended—and it must end—his absence would only hurt the girls.

Her arguments against considering a second marriage failed to stir her resolve as they always had before. She knew Jared would never hurt her, would never ask anything of her she wasn't willing to give. He lived out his Christianity, and in the short time she'd known him, almost from the beginning, he'd found a door into her life she hadn't realized she'd left unlocked. Or perhaps his laughter and tenderness had been the key—

"Mom?"

Sharon jumped a little at the unexpected sound of Mindy beside her. She hadn't heard the door open.

"I'm sorry. I ate my potatoes and turkey, but do I hafta eat the cake?"

Sharon let out a laughing sob and rolled over to embrace her daughter. Mindy's arms squeezed her back just as hard.

"I guess I should've known better than to expect my kids to do cartwheels about a cake with vegetables in it, huh?"

Mindy giggled.

"Maybe there are some pudding cups still in the fridge."

"Chocolate?"

"Unless Andy found them, all that are probably left are the swirls."

"I like swirls!"

At last, Sharon had hit upon something her daughter liked.

"Moppet?" Sharon addressed Mindy by her special nickname. "Mama's sorry, too. It's been a rough week, but I shouldn't have taken it out on you guys."

"I understand." Mindy looked at her with wise eyes, and Sharon believed she understood more than Sharon was willing to say.

"Let's go get those pudding cups, shall we?"

"Yeah—let's!"

They were all sitting around the table in harmony as a family again, giggling over a joke Kitty had just told and halfway through the plastic pudding cups when the doorbell rang. Kitty rocketed off the chair before Sharon could stop her.

"I wonder who could be here on a holiday," Sharon mused aloud. "Everyone I know had plans."

Kitty came to the kitchen door, her eyes sparkling and her smile as big as Christmas morning. Jared entered behind her, his eyes just as lively, his smile a bit uncertain. A thought startled Sharon's mind: Now, her Thanksgiving was complete.

ten

Jared hoped he wasn't intruding on their holiday, but he saw by the food on the plates they had just finished dinner. At least the family, except for Andy, looked happy to see him.

"I just swung by. I gave the nieces and nephews a ride in the sleigh earlier and thought that while we still had daylight, you guys might like to take a ride."

He barely got out the last few words amid the little girls' squeals. Both girls shot up from the table and clustered around their mother.

"Can we, Mom?" Mindy begged.

"Can we?" Kitty repeated.

"Pleeease," both of them cried, before beginning another round of begging.

Sharon laughed and shook her head. "All right, all right, just give me room to breathe."

"Yea!" they shouted in unison before darting from the room. "Let's go see the sleigh!"

"Coats, hats, and gloves!" Sharon called, but they disappeared out the door.

"Once the outside air hits them, they'll remember," he assured. "What about you?" he asked when she remained seated. "Aren't you coming?"

"I probably shouldn't be getting out right now. I woke up with a tickle in my throat and can't afford a cold."

Jared felt disappointed; he had looked forward to this since he'd gotten the idea to hitch up Tamany and Treacle. He wondered if the suggestion that she wrap her neck in a thick scarf would sound too selfish and decided it would.

"That's too bad. I hope you feel better soon."

"I'm feeling better than I was. I just don't want to make it worse."

In the background, the door slammed, the sound of running feet and laughing complaints about the cold heralding the girls' reentrance. A door creaked open in the background, and Jared assumed they were fetching their outerwear.

He glanced at Andy, already sure of the boy's answer but feeling he should ask. "Would you like to take a ride in the sleigh?"

"Do Martians inhabit the earth?"

His gaze steady, he sensed a rude refusal. "No."

"There's your answer." The boy's eyes glimmered with their usual dislike.

"Andy," Sharon warned.

"No. . .thanks," he added, grudgingly.

Jared withheld a sigh, wondering what it would take for Andy to cease considering him as the enemy. "I talked to Hugh yesterday." He directed his words to Sharon while Andy started his third pudding cup. Two empty cups sat in front of him. "I was at the store picking up a few things for my mother and I ran into Hugh. He asked about you guys, said he wouldn't mind some help at the farm. Mentioned Andy and asked if I thought he'd be interested."

"He got rid of Caramel," Andy sulked.

"Well, he did say she seems to be doing fine. Apparently, she's been visiting the farm recently."

This got the boy's attention.

"My moose calf?" he asked, though Jared could see it was killing him to talk in a sociable way with him. "Caramel's been coming around Hugh's farm?"

"Yup, according to Hugh. He's been monitoring the calf's

progress and still feeds it when it comes around. With winter coming on, he's short of help."

"Mom? Can I?"

Sharon's brow creased in worry. "He's only twelve," she said to Jared.

"I'm almost thirteen, Mom."

"And Hugh's farm is ten miles away," she continued as if Andy hadn't spoken. "What can Hugh be thinking?"

"Twelve-going-on-thirteen isn't so young," Jared assured, thinking of some of the jobs he'd had at that age. "It's only for several hours on the weekends."

"Mom, please?"

"What about school, Andy? That comes first."

"I'll study real hard and ace all my tests. I already have been, and the stuff we're learning now is so easy, it's boring. Please, Mom."

She sighed. "I'll have to think about this, Andy. I can't give you an answer right now."

Andy didn't argue with her, his expression that of a boy walking on thin ice. He rose from his chair, picked up his dishes, and stacked others on top, then took them all to the sink.

Jared acknowledged he probably should have discussed the matter with Sharon in private. If nothing else came from this, at least she wouldn't have to deal with Andy's misbehavior, what with the buttering-up job he witnessed. He watched Andy gather the garbage in preparation for taking it out, and from the perceptive smile of amusement Sharon sent Jared, he understood the boy's voluntary help wasn't a normal occurrence.

The girls appeared, bundled like miniature green and pink snowmen, and Jared escorted them out to the sleigh. First they insisted on petting Tamany and the matching bay, Treacle, their mittened hands stroking their velvet noses and necks.

Tamany nickered and gave a slight toss of her mane, enjoying the attention.

Once he'd tucked them under the blanket and they took off, the girls squealed to hear the sound of the bells on the harness jingle, and Jared chuckled at their excitement.

"You girls act like you've never been on a sleigh ride before."

"We haven't."

Their answer surprised him. He was so accustomed to the sleigh that the novelty of the event had worn off long ago. But through the girls' eyes, he experienced the ride as if for the first time.

Mindy and Kitty squealed and waved to any passersby they met, those on foot and in their cars, as if they were princesses in a parade acknowledging their devoted subjects. Jared noted that cheerful smiles and amused waves always answered their exuberant welcomes. The holidays brought out the best in everyone. Their town was friendly, but especially around the holidays, Jared felt like he inhabited a Norman Rockwell town in a Currier and Ives setting.

He drove Tamany and Treacle past their white-steepled church, which stood amid the snowy landscape near a backdrop of twilight blue sky. A huge evergreen, over two stories tall, stood like a sentinel at the front and toward the side of the building. Strings of golden Christmas lights glimmered in its boughs, repeating the soft yellow glow of the church's windows.

He had hoped to share such a peaceful, romantic setting with Sharon and chuckled wryly that his plans, again, had backfired. But he enjoyed her girls' company and took them away from the buildings of town and over the hills of Goosebury.

"If you girls don't stop all that squealing," he said with a smile, "you might not have voices for the Christmas program. It's not all that far away, remember."

His mild, amused warning didn't faze them one bit.

"Let's sing a song!" Kitty insisted.

"What kind of song?" Jared asked.

"A sleigh song!"

"Yeah! Like the one you made up the day we met you," Mindy added.

"A sleigh song," Jared muttered in reflection. "Okay, how about this? Drive, drive, drive your sleigh, over the ice and snow—two squealing girls, giggling and waving, a-sleighing we will go!"

The girls giggled again, and soon they both joined in at the top of their lungs in countless rounds, broken up by even more giggling. And Jared had thought his nieces were bad when it came to uncontrollable laughter!

He grinned at their silliness, glad they were having such a fun time. He didn't regret following through with the sleigh ride, even if it hadn't gone according to plan.

Once he delivered the girls safely home, they jumped out, thanking him, and hurried inside. They left the front door wide, and unsure if he should go inside or not, he peeked his head around the partition.

"Hello?"

Sharon caught sight of him as she came from the kitchen. Laughter sailed down the hallway.

"Come in. It sounds like they had a good time."

"Yeah." He stepped inside and shut the door against the cold. "So did I."

Her eyes stayed on him a moment, looked away, then back. "Would you like some coffee? I have carrot cake, too."

"I've never tried it, but sure."

They headed to the kitchen. Kitty and Mindy ran out from the hallway, minus coats and mittens, and almost mowed Jared down.

"Thank you," Kitty said, wrapping her arms around his

middle. "I had the bestest time!"

Sharon shook her head in amusement and popped the girls' overlooked stocking caps off. "It's time for both of you to get ready for bed."

"Can't we stay up since it's vacation?" Mindy pleaded. "Please!"

With a tolerant smile, Sharon let out a resigned breath. "One hour. But go play in your room. I need to talk to Jared alone."

"Yea!" The girls squealed and raced away.

"Quietly!" she called after them.

Jared noted the sound of their bedroom door clicking softly closed and couldn't prevent a grin. A grin that disappeared the moment he caught sight of Sharon's more somber expression.

"Am I in trouble?" he half joked.

"Maybe. Let's talk in the kitchen."

Jared followed, now almost dreading the next few minutes.

❧

Sharon poured them both coffee. She cut them each a slice of cake and sat down across the table from him, setting the plates down as she did.

"Jared, I know you're only trying to help with Andy, but next time, please wait until you can discuss it with me. I'm not sure what to do about that job situation; Andy has been a handful lately, but now. . ."

"You're right; I made a mistake in doing that. I didn't think before I spoke, and I'm sorry."

Amazed, Sharon studied him. She had never known a man who admitted to being wrong. When she had tried to talk to Mark about similar matters, he'd gone on the defensive and then, too often, the offensive.

"But now that we're alone, I'd like to continue our discussion," he went on.

She realized he was asking her permission, and she nodded.

"I think this job would be good for Andy. I know"—he raised his hand as though to curb a comeback—"I'm one to talk since I don't have kids. But I speak from experience. I was about Andy's age when my dad had had enough of my pranks, which had really gotten out of control by then, and he made me get a summer job. I threw newspapers—not much, but it helped me learn to be responsible and kept me out of trouble. I still had chores on the farm, but this gave me a sense of independence, and earning some of my own money helped me better appreciate what I had. I had a lot, but at age twelve, kids often don't realize that."

She appreciated his sincerity. "You make a good case. I'll admit once you left I had pretty well decided the answer would be a no, but I'll rethink my decision."

"Glad to hear it. If you decide in favor of the idea and ever need someone to give him a lift—if my aunts' car fails or you have to work—give me a call."

Jared never failed to astonish her with his thoughtfulness. It was too bad Andy didn't realize what a support he had in Jared.

"I'll remember that."

He smiled and took a bite of cake. He looked at it, his expression neither delighted nor disgusted.

"You don't have to eat it if you don't want to. It hasn't been the flavor of the day here."

"It's okay."

"Are you sure? I can get you some doughnuts to go with your coffee instead." She had half-risen from her chair when he reached across the table and put his fingers to her arm to stop her movement. The contact, though brief, burned through her sweater.

"Sharon, it's fine." He studied her. "This is the second time you've worried about my reaction to the food. What gives?"

She opened her mouth to speak, then closed it and took a sip of coffee, sorting out her thoughts. "Mark was very demanding when it came to his meals. If something was the least bit off, he let me know he didn't like it. It's one reason I quit cooking from scratch." She left it at that, and from Jared's expression, he understood what she didn't say.

"Sharon, I'm not Mark."

"I know that." She attempted a smile. "You're nothing like him. It's just that sometimes. . ." She looked down at her cake. "I can't help it if memories interfere with the present. I've received counseling, and I have a support group. But it takes time to heal. It's been years, I know, but I really thought when Mark accepted the Lord and I saw that change in him, that once he got out of prison we'd have that second chance at the life I always wanted." She detested the tears that rose to her eyes and brushed them away, giving Jared a bright smile. "But obviously it just wasn't meant to be."

"I'm sorry it didn't happen like you dreamt it would." His eyes were nothing but sincere, and she believed he really meant it. "But sometimes when we lose sight of a dream we hoped for, God ends up giving us something better."

"I know. That's what Leslie said." She gave a soft laugh. "I have my friends, my kids, a good place to live, and a job I love, with employers who are more like surrogate grandmothers than true managers." She laughed again. "A lot of women would love to live my life."

He grinned, though his eyes remained serious. "You do have a lot, but I feel God has more for you."

His words made her a bit nervous, and she focused on her cake, eating a bite. She wondered if he meant himself, and if he still harbored some pipe dream that she would consider him as more than a friend.

"Can I ask a question?" He sounded hesitant.

She gave a noncommittal nod for him to go on.

"Tell me if it's none of my business, and I'll understand. But something has been bothering me, and I'd really like to know. Why'd you stay with him all that time?"

"You mean, why didn't I leave after the first time he beat me up?"

He winced. "Yeah."

She exhaled a deep sigh, drinking more of her coffee before trying to explain. "My stepfather was abusive to my mom, too, and verbally abusive to me and my sister. By the time I met Mark, I'd already formed a low opinion of myself. So when he added his insults along with the smacks, I grew to believe I really did deserve everything I got."

She shrugged. "You probably think that sounds crazy, but when you're told lies about yourself all your life, before long you believe them. When he'd come back, repentant and in tears, I felt like I had no choice but to take him in, that it really was my fault that I'd made him so angry, and that I was the one who needed to do most of the changing. Of course, I know differently now. But it took a lot of patience from some dear Christian friends to help me see that I wasn't at fault and that Mark was the one with the problem."

"I'm glad you sought help and have grown from the experience," he said. "You're an amazing woman, Sharon."

Her heart quickened at the quiet manner in which he said the words as well as the way his gaze grew so intent on her own.

She stood suddenly on the pretext of going for napkins, needing to break away from his soul-shaking eyes.

"I should go."

She pivoted in surprise to see he'd also risen from his chair. "You just got here."

"Yeah, but it's late, and I have plenty to do over the next

few weeks both at the farm and with the program. I called a practice for both this Friday afternoon and Saturday, in case the girls didn't tell you."

"They did." She hesitated. "I'm not sure why I never asked before, but do you live on your parents' farm?"

"Not exactly, not in their house. I have my own place close by, on the land. Nothing much to talk about. A cabin, to sleep; I'm not there often." He chuckled. "I'm usually at Mom's to eat, or at my aunts' or at one of my brother's or sister's houses. They all insist on keeping me well fed."

She smiled at the thought that his family took good care of him; she wondered if his compassion was a hereditary trait.

"Thanks for the coffee." He stood watching her, as if undecided about approaching for a handshake or a hug—she didn't know which, but she saw the desire in his eyes and sensed he waited for a signal from her. Uneasy, she lowered her gaze to the napkins she held, then looked back up at him. He gave her a slight, almost disappointed grin. "No need to walk me to the door. Good night, Sharon."

She watched as he left the kitchen. Everything in her ached to call him back, but she only returned to her chair and stared at her cake. The front door clicked closed, and silence settled thick around her.

eleven

Sharon sat on the pew next to Leslie, who held Marena on her lap while Blaine held a sleeping baby Paula over his shoulder. Carly sat on the other side, with Nate next to her, his arm around his wife.

"Just think, in a few years, I'll be one of the proud mamas watching my little girl perform." Leslie kissed Marena's hair. "Time goes so fast."

"Yes, it does," Sharon agreed. "And after having to whip up an angel costume and a wise-man costume, it seems to go even faster. It's a good thing I had Loretta's help. She's an expert when it comes to getting sequins to stay on the material *and* look decent."

"Those two really love you and your kids, Angel." Carly's eyes gleamed. "And unless I miss my guess, I'm certain someone else does, too."

Sharon knew she referred to Jared and looked his way. He caught sight of her from where he stood at the front and gave a friendly nod. Feeling the blush clear to her toes, she returned the greeting.

"Like I said," Carly mused, leaving the statement unfinished. Her eyes danced with mischievous delight.

Sharon quickly changed the subject, pointing out costumes as more children approached the stage. The heavenly chorus, she assumed from reading the program in her hand, though they wore silver robes and didn't have wings like the angels. She had spent the greater part of one day off from work, making the gauzelike, sequined wings she'd wrapped around wire hangers and trying to get them to fasten right and not hang lopsided on Kitty's costume. Mindy's wise-man outfit hadn't been half as difficult to put together.

The lights went down, the only electric light remaining a soft spotlight above where the pulpit usually stood. At the edge of three steps that led to the altar, candles glowed and flickered in tall, ornate golden stands. The wooden stable Ted and a few other men had built stood in the center as the shepherds flocked around it.

Jill played the organ, and the program unfolded without a hitch. Mindy almost forgot one of her two lines but recovered after only seconds. Kitty looked adorable in her angel costume, and Sharon smiled with pride as she watched her daughters perform.

"Did you make those wings?" Leslie asked.

Sharon nodded.

"They look like they could have been bought from a craft store. That's some amazing work."

"I've dabbled in crafts ever since high school," she whispered back. "That's one reason I applied for a sales position at A'Bric & A'Brac. When I saw they dealt in homemade crafts, I fell in love with the place."

The finale began, and the wise men bowed before the baby Jesus, played by Carly and Nate's baby Mali. No boys had been born in the congregation within the last year to take the role, and Carly's baby was reputed to have the best temperament. Tonight, however, she presented another side to her personality.

Mali squealed and grabbed one of the wise men's fake beards, bringing it to her mouth. The band holding it behind the boy's ears stretched. He leaned far into the manger as his wise man companion, Mindy, tried to disentangle Mali's fingers from the cottony wool.

"See." Andy leaned up from the pew behind Sharon to whisper

in her ear. "I told you they shouldn't have gotten a girl."

At that moment, Mali let go of the beard, and the elastic band snapped back into place, stinging the poor wise man in the jaw.

"Ow!" he cried, rubbing his chin.

Jared's reaction came immediately, as he directed the heavenly chorus to begin the final carol of "Gloria."

Sharon tried hard not to laugh. By the way their shoulders shook, a number of the rest of the congregation dealt with the same problem.

The burst of singing made Mali cry. The children froze, uncertain what to do. They looked back and forth from the baby to Jared, who silently directed from the wings, and then to the audience. Mindy suddenly bent down and picked up Mali, holding her close and jiggling her while the chorus ended their final *gloria*s.

"Trust Mali to steal the spotlight," Carly said in an aside to Leslie and Sharon after the lights went up and everyone had been dismissed. "That girl is going to be an actress. Mark my words." She hurried up to the front to collect her daughter.

Mindy and Kitty ran up to Sharon, their eyes gleaming.

"Did you hear me sing, Mama?" Kitty wanted to know.

"I messed up," Mindy said, "but then I remembered my line. Do you think anyone else noticed? Did you like it?"

"Both of you were wonderful," Sharon assured, hugging her daughters.

"They really were," Jared said, and Sharon looked up in surprise, not realizing he'd joined them. "I was proud of both of them, and did you notice how Mindy saved the program?" He winked at the girl.

"Sorry about Mali's theatrics," Nate said, shaking hands with Jared. Jill and Ted joined them.

"Well, when a baby is part of the cast, I imagine you have

to expect such things." Jared shrugged it off with a grin. "But unless any new babies are born between now and next year, I imagine they'll have to go back to a doll."

"As a matter of fact. . ." Jill's face went pink.

Sharon looked at her. "Jill? You're not serious."

"Too right. Remember when I thought I couldn't have kids, before Titus came along?"

"I remember! And now God is giving you a triple blessing," Leslie enthused, hugging Jill.

"Too right," Ted echoed his wife's Australian slang, beaming like he'd just been given the news.

Everyone laughed, and the couple received congratulations all around. Sharon was thrilled for Jill but couldn't help feel a twinge of envy. She'd always wanted a lot of children and would have loved to have another baby. But that meant marriage, and she wasn't ready for that. She corrected the surprisingly vague thought—*never* would be ready for that.

"So I might become one of those stage mamas," Jill laughed. "Be warned, Jared."

"Well, that's great—I think," he joked. "But I'm resigning as children's choir director."

"What?" Sharon asked. "How come?"

"I only volunteered for the job until Pastor could find someone more qualified, and I just don't think I'm cut out for it."

"Sharon could always take over," Leslie said.

"Sharon?" Jared glanced her way in confusion.

Sharon sent Leslie a sharp look, and Leslie glanced at the floor. "Oops. Sorry. I forgot."

"Do you sing?" Jared asked.

"No," Sharon said. "I don't," she stressed, looking at Leslie. "And I have no experience teaching choir, either."

"What's this I hear about you quitting, Jared?" A young

man similar to Jared in looks came up and slapped him on the back.

"Hello, Brandon. Where's the family?"

"Darla's helping Rex out of his costume, and Mom and Dad are talking to the Abernathys."

Leslie perked up. "I need to talk to Nana before she leaves. I'll talk to you guys later."

The newcomer looked directly at Sharon. "Since Jared seems to have misplaced his manners—hi, I'm Brandon, Jared's brother. You must be Sharon. I've heard a lot about you."

"Hello." She shook his hand, not failing to notice the glint of mischief in his eyes and how Jared's face suddenly flushed.

"Sorry, I was about to do that," Jared said.

"I just came over to tell you what a great job you did with the program," Brandon told him. "You deserve whatever you put on your Christmas list this year, and I imagine I know what'll be at the very top." He chuckled as if sharing a private joke.

Jared turned even redder. "They're serving hot cider and cookies in the kitchen. Why don't you go fill your mouth with some?" he suggested.

Brandon laughed as if Jared had told a big joke, but Sharon saw Jared wasn't amused. And suddenly she understood what was number one on his list. Brandon's curious glances in her direction, along with Jared's focus elsewhere, convinced her Brandon's comment had to do with her.

"We should be going," she said, putting a hand on each of her daughters' shoulders.

"You're not staying for the party?" Jill asked.

"Not tonight."

"Mo—omm," Mindy complained.

"You still have school tomorrow. School doesn't let out for vacation until the end of this week." She wondered if she appeared as nervous as she sounded.

"But it's still early!"

"Sorry, Min. Not tonight. You and Andy both also have homework. Night all." She included the entire group in her hurried good-bye, while herding her girls to the door and Loretta and Josephine's car, which was finally in good running order. "Come along, Andy," she called to her son, who talked outside with a boy his age. She felt a little foolish for making such a fast escape, but couldn't help herself.

Feeling bad for denying Mindy and Kitty a well-deserved party, she stopped at a fast-food place and bought everyone a hot chocolate with whipped cream. Once they arrived home, she pulled out a bag of chocolate chip cookies, and they had a short, private celebration before she shooed Andy and Mindy off to finish their homework and Kitty off to bed.

The girls seemed satisfied with the substitute party, but Sharon couldn't stop feeling on edge.

"What's wrong with me?" she muttered, threading her fingers through her hair, her elbows on the table as she rested her head in her hands.

She couldn't even be sure Brandon implied Jared still hoped for a relationship with her; she'd only assumed it. She had known how Jared felt from the start, though he agreed to her stipulation of "just friends." Sometimes, though, when she looked into his eyes, she sensed he desired more. What had scared her and made her run like a frightened doe that evening was that she had begun to desire the same.

❧

"Thanks a ton," Jared mumbled to his brother the moment Sharon fled.

"Hey, I didn't mean anything by it. I didn't realize she'd be so fidgety and would take off like that; I'm sorry, dude." Brandon looked the slightest bit uneasy, and Jared relented. After all, he'd never told any of his brothers the details of his and Sharon's strange relationship, or more accurately, their lack of one.

"Let's get some of that cider and I'll explain things. But only if you promise not to use it against me in the future, especially when we're in public."

"Now, would I do that to you?"

"Yup," Jared came back without hesitation. "I'm surprised Darla lets you out in public."

"I really thought you two were together, or I wouldn't have said a word."

Their trek to the church cafeteria was slow; many parents and their excited future stars stopped Jared to congratulate him on the program's rousing success. They'd either forgotten Mali's finale, or maybe they thought her impromptu performance added to the program.

Once they collected cups of cider from a smiling Mrs. Moorehead, Jared told his brother everything since his first meeting with Sharon. He didn't divulge those things Sharon had confided in him, except to say she'd endured some tough situations that made it difficult for her to trust.

His brother stared at him.

"What?" Jared asked.

"I'm still trying to get past the fact that you have *finally* found The One." With two fingers of each hand, he made quote marks in the air.

"Forget I said anything." Irritated with what he felt would result in another round of ribbing, Jared shook his head and took a sip of cider.

"No, wait. I meant that in a good way." His brother's expression *seemed* earnest. "You always stuck to your guns in this, unaffected by anything the family had to say, and Tom, Josh, and I have given you a hard time, even if it was all in fun. But hearing you tell how it happened—and that it all went the exact way you felt God said it would—right down to the smallest detail—man, Jared. That's awesome."

"It is, isn't it? Now I only have to convince Sharon," he reminded dryly.

"Yeah, well, I don't know. You've trusted God all this time, so why stop now? I don't think He'd let you down after bringing you this far."

"I know. I just have to be patient." He sighed. He was certainly getting a lengthy lesson in patience.

"You could always use the old 'absence makes the heart grow fonder' bit."

"What are you talking about?"

"I did it with Darla. She acted like she wanted nothing to do with me at first, though our friends made me think otherwise and I'd catch her looking my way. So I got the idea that if I acted disinterested maybe she'd change her tune. Even when my buddies told me she kept searching for me and asked questions, I stayed hidden. After a month, she caved." Brandon grinned. "I still hide from her at the pool hall or at the lake fishing with the guys, but now it's only when I need to get away."

"Not only does the whole concept sound immature, it sounds cold-blooded." Jared eyed his brother in disbelief.

"It worked." Brandon shrugged.

Jared shook his head, always amazed to what new lows his youngest brother would stoop. No wonder his parents tried to keep him away from the tourists. "Well, I won't have time for socializing after tonight. Things are getting busier on the farm, and you won't have time for any games of hide-and-seek from Darla either."

"Okay, okay. So what do you plan to do about Sharon? You going to take my advice?"

"Giving her a little space might not be a bad idea with the way things have gone between us lately. But the last thing I plan to do is hide from her."

twelve

Sharon wondered if Jared was hiding from her. That idea seemed preposterous when she considered it, but since the night of the Christmas program, she'd barely seen a trace of him. She assumed he'd been busy with work, but except for the two times she'd called asking him to give Andy a lift to Hugh's farm when the sisters' car died, Sharon hadn't seen Jared much at all.

She told herself it was silly to feel wounded by his lack of company; the two times she did see him, he was as friendly as always, and she knew she was being ridiculous to view his absence as a slight.

On Christmas Eve morning, she and the kids took the two-hour bus ride to her mom's. Her stepfather was gone for the day, something for which she was grateful, though her mom didn't mention where he was.

"You look good, Mom," Sharon said as she helped her mother make turkey sandwiches. The girls sat planted in front of the television in the next room, watching an animated Christmas special, and Andy stood outside tossing a ball to Brambles, her stepfather's mutt.

The dark circles under her mom's eyes made her appear tired, but she did look better than the last time Sharon had seen her, at Mark's funeral. On that day, she'd had bruises.

"I didn't want to say anything with the kids in the room," her mom murmured under her breath, "but Garth is in rehab."

"Rehab?" Sharon almost dropped the mayonnaise jar as she set it down.

Her mother nodded. "After what happened with. . ." She hesitated, her eyes darting to Sharon, then to the slices of bread laid out, as if realizing she had brought up a touchy subject.

"It's okay, Mom," Sharon assured her. "You mean after Mark was killed in prison."

"Yes, well, not long after that, he came to me after one of his drunks and told me he wanted help. I'd never seen him like that. He cried—actually cried like a baby. He didn't seek professional help until last month, though. He tried quitting on his own. It didn't work."

"Why didn't you tell me all this before?" Sharon stared at her mom in disbelief.

"I didn't want to bother you, what with all you've been through." Her mom bit her lip, uneasy.

Sharon withheld a sigh, recognizing the old feeling of unworthiness in her mom's eyes, a feeling Sharon was conquering in her own life with the Lord's help.

"I'm glad Garth woke up and is getting the help he needs," she said, forcing a smile.

She tried not to feel cheated but felt a twinge of selfishness. Why couldn't Mark have sought help before he threw his life away by stabbing Leslie with his vengeful plan of getting even with Dear Granny? That he found help during his last year in prison brought some comfort. Nor could she look at her life with him as wasted. It had brought her the blessings of her three children.

"Will you come home with me to Goosebury?" Sharon asked. "You shouldn't be here alone."

"This is my home, Sharon. I can't leave." Her mom smiled. "I'll be fine."

Sharon didn't doubt that; her mom was made of strong stuff, though Sharon wished she would open her mind and heart to talk about God. So far, she'd shown polite disinterest the few times Sharon had brought up the topic. Sharon hoped her mother wouldn't be upset with her gift.

That night as they opened presents and the children soon became immersed in playing with the toys their grandmother gave each of them, Sharon's mom looked at the book in her lap. Along with it, Sharon had given her a blue cashmere, button-down sweater, which her mom had immediately draped around her shoulders. But she only stared at the jacket cover of *God's Answer to a Life without Fear,* her expression blank.

"A very kind woman gave me that book a few years ago, not long before the police arrested Mark. She helps her granddaughter, a friend of mine, write an advice column for my local paper," she added when her mom didn't respond. She omitted Leslie's and Mrs. Abernathy's names, knowing they wanted their cowriting profession as the advice columnist Dear Granny to remain secret. "That book has helped me, and I want you to have it now."

"Honey, I can't take your book."

"No, Mom, really, it's okay. When this woman gave it to me, she told me someone first gave it to her, and it helped her face her fears. She said she thinks it's a book that should be passed along, which is why she gave it to me. And now I want to do the same. With you." She omitted saying it also brought her closer to God. Such an admission might cause her mother to lose any possible interest in reading it.

"Something like a chain book?" Her mom lifted her brows and smiled, showing the first bit of spirited amusement she'd exhibited all day.

Sharon chuckled. "I guess you could call it that."

The remainder of the evening went well. The kids seemed more relaxed and happy than on previous visits, and Sharon didn't doubt Garth's absence made them more secure. His verbal abuse had created general unease, and Sharon ended each visit within a few hours. This evening, however, she accepted her mom's invitation to stay the night.

The girls giggled at the spontaneous decision and thought it a great adventure that they had no clothes and each had to wear one of their granny's gowns, which hung on them like angel robes. After minutes of bouncing up and down on the feather mattress with a pillow fight following, Sharon read them "The Night Before Christmas" and at last got them calm enough to sleep.

Their heads nestled in their pillows, both girls looked up at Sharon from the guest room's double bed. Their golden hair was tousled from their play, their eyes drowsy from the fun they'd had.

"What do you think Jared is doing for Christmas?" Kitty wanted to know as Sharon tucked the thick, down blanket around her and Mindy.

The mention of the man she'd been trying to forget made Sharon's heart give a strange little leap.

"I imagine he's with his family, like we are."

Kitty thought a moment. "But he *is* like family. So why didn't he come over, too?"

Sharon studied her daughter with concerned alarm. "Honey," she said gently, "Jared's not family. He's just a good friend."

"That's not what I heard Mrs. Loretta and Miss Josephine say," she insisted. "They were all happy that Jared found the woman he was gonna marry." Then, as if Sharon wouldn't understand, she went on. "They meant you, Mama."

Sharon felt her heart catch. "They told you that?"

Kitty averted her eyes. "Well, no. I just heard them."

"You were eavesdropping," Sharon scolded. "What have I told you about that?"

"I wasn't trying to be bad," Kitty insisted. "I went to get some cookies, and they were talking in the kitchen. I heard them."

"Are you gonna marry Jared, Mama?" Mindy wanted to know.

Sharon's mouth dropped open in shock at the blatant question. Both the girls' eyes sparkled with hope. The sooner she got such dancing sugarplum ideas out of their heads, the better. Best to squelch all visions concerning any such notion.

"Goodness, no. I never plan to marry again."

"Why not?" Kitty wanted to know. "Miss Josephine said the Lord said man shouldn't live alone."

"She told you that?"

"No, she told Mrs. Loretta."

"Well, I'm not alone; I have you two. And Andy."

"And then Mrs. Loretta answered that she agreed with the plan God gave Jared, since Paul said in the Bible young widows are supposed to marry," Mindy shot back. "It's in the Bible," she repeated for good measure.

"You were listening, too?"

"I went to see what Kitty was doing."

Sharon crossed her arms over her chest, unsmiling, and surveyed her two mischievous matchmakers. "I've raised you girls better than that. You better watch out with this disobedience, or Santa might just decide to skip over our house tonight." She'd already told them Santa wouldn't come to their grandmother's; the sleepover had been a spur of the moment thing, and the kids' presents were at home, still unwrapped.

"But Mama," Mindy insisted, not fazed by the mild threat, "if God says you shouldn't stay single, doesn't that mean you're supposed to marry someone? And God's a whole lot more important than Santa. That's what you said. So doesn't that mean you're not obeying God? And isn't that even worse?"

This conversation was spinning out of control too fast for Sharon's peace of mind. Both girls now looked worried, and Sharon realized Mindy wasn't trying to be disrespectful.

"Okay, that's enough chitchat for one night," she said, managing a smile. "Tomorrow is Christmas, and it'll be here before you know it."

."But Mama. . ."

Sharon rose from the mattress, deposited quick kisses on their brows, and turned out the light. In the attic room, she found Andy sound asleep on the recliner in front of an ancient TV that aired an old black-and-white Christmas movie. Relieved that she wouldn't need to field any additional questions, she turned off the set. She tucked him snugly inside the blankets and kissed his forehead, then headed downstairs to work on a scenic Christmas puzzle with her mom. Hundreds of colorful pieces lay scattered across the dining table. Soft instrumental Christmas music played from the stereo. Her mom was so involved in working the puzzle, she barely spoke, which meant Sharon had a lot of time to think.

As Sharon tried to interlock matching colors, Mindy's fears wouldn't vacate her mind. Did such a verse exist in the Bible, or were the girls just creating more mischief? Sharon hadn't read enough of the New Testament to know, though she'd read bits and pieces here and there, centering on the readings Pastor Neil taught his congregation. For her own private worship time, she used a devotional that directed her to certain scriptures each day.

What if such a verse really did exist? Jared was everything Mark hadn't been: sweet, funny, kind, affectionate. She enjoyed spending time with Jared and missed him. Yet even if he did still have interest in her—although his absence seemed to prove otherwise—and even if the verse Mindy cited was genuine, even then, Sharon wasn't sure she could break her resolve regarding her decision never to marry.

❧

As days passed into weeks, Jared remained busy on his family's farm. The winter had been quiet, with the usual blizzards that snowed them in and chores that multiplied. Jared enjoyed his assigned task of tending to the farm animals, keeping them snug in the barn, while outside the snow fell often and deep. When none of the family was present and Jared was the sole human occupant of the barn, he often found himself singing. At least the animals seemed to enjoy his performances.

The days had grown warmer at spring's approach, the nights frozen, the perfect time for sugaring. The process could last from a matter of days to weeks, depending on the weather. Each spring, new tapholes needed to be bored into tree trunks, taps and hollow tubes needed to be inserted, and Jared, along with many of the men in his family, had spent the past days readying trees for gathering sap.

For the trees within easy access, they used the old-fashioned, bucket-collecting method. But for the sugar bush on the hill-sides, they attached plastic tubes to the taps, which formed a network of tubing that allowed the thawed sap to flow to a huge storage tank near the sugarhouse. Today, Jared sang under his breath, not caring that he had company.

"You seem in a good mood," Tom said as Jared brushed Tamany, readying her for the day's ride, along with Treacle.

"I'm bringing Sharon and her kids to the farm. They want to see how the sugaring is done."

"And of course that's your sole reason for playing chauffeur," Tom joked.

"You know," Jared said with a good-natured grin, "you're not so big now that I can't whip you, little brother."

"Don't be so sure." Tom patted his big stomach, which hung an inch over his belt. "I can still wrestle you to the ground any day."

"Well, it's fortunate for you we won't see that theory tested. I have to make tracks. I told her I'd be there by noon."

"All joking aside, how'd you get her to change her mind about meeting the folks?"

"I don't really know. I saw her at church last Sunday, and when she asked what I'd been doing, I told her it was sugaring time. Kitty asked if she could come and see, and Sharon said they could. I have to admit, I'm still baffled, since I wasn't expecting her to agree."

"Maybe you're getting to her."

"Uh, yup. Sure." He waved his brother's comment off and hitched Tamany and Treacle to the wagon. After three months, eight days, and twelve hours of hardly seeing Sharon, he looked forward to the prospect, but he doubted she had missed him. As he drove to her house, however, his brother's words reverberated in his mind, and Jared wondered if Tom could be right. Had Sharon thawed toward him? She had seemed happy to see him and talk with him outside of church.

Once she opened the door to his knock, the thought entered his mind that she looked like a breath of fresh air. Wearing white and a shade of blue that matched her eyes, she dazzled. The girls jumped at him, hugging him. Andy stood nearby and stared at Jared, and to his surprise, Jared sensed less animosity in the boy. Ever since Sharon had bought a used car, she'd been toting Andy back and forth to his weekend job, but Andy had the day off since Hugh's family had gone out of town. She had offered to drive to the farm, but Jared insisted he would pick them up in his horse-drawn sleigh instead.

This Saturday's weather was perfect for a sleigh ride. The sun shone from a pale blue sky, the days had warmed, and the snow of a few hours ago had stopped falling.

Once they drove onto his family's land, past the sign that announced CRISP SUGARWOODS to welcome them, Sharon stared in wide-eyed shock. The closer they came to the farmhouse, the more stunned she appeared as she looked around at the distant hillsides of snow-flocked trees.

"Everything okay?" he asked.

"I thought you meant your family had a farm. You never told me you meant a *farm*. I had no idea your parents' place was this big." Her voice squeaked in her nervousness. "How big is it, anyway?"

"It's 525 acres," he said, wondering why he hadn't brought it up before. His family's wealth and his own interests in the maple sugar farm had never been a problem or something he broadcasted. It just—was. He had mentioned tourists visited year round, so he'd thought Sharon would have figured out the place was big. "Crisp Sugarwoods has been in the family for generations, since the 1800s."

His parents' two-story farmhouse appeared in the distance, and he sensed by her jittery behavior that Sharon wanted to bolt from the sleigh.

"Sharon, it's okay," he said in an undertone so the kids in the back couldn't hear. The girls were busy pointing out to each other the different features of the farm. "My family members are good, plain country folk. Nothing scary about them—well, except maybe for my brothers." He winked, and she seemed to relax a margin.

"I'm surprised with a house that big you'd want to live in a cabin all by yourself," she remarked, her eyes taking in every inch of the wide brown house which stood out against the snow-covered surroundings.

"Let's just say I'm a man who likes my independence."

"So." She cleared her throat. "Where's your cabin?"

"On the other side of the sugarhouse, beyond those trees," he added when she craned her neck to look. "My parents keep their farmhouse private from the area where we let tourists roam. I'll show you my cabin later."

"Oh, I didn't mean—" Her face grew redder, but the sight of

a few members of his family coming out of the house to meet them interrupted whatever she'd been about to say.

For the next few minutes, Jared introduced Sharon and her family to his mom; two of his sisters-in-law, Darla and Carol; and some of his nephews and nieces. His brothers and father were busy on other areas of the farm, and once he and Sharon entered the house, Jared saw a majority of his small nieces and nephews sat at the huge dining table, finishing lunch. Bless his mom, she took Sharon and her kids right into her heart, making them feel comfortable with her easy conversation. In relief, Jared watched Sharon relax, her smiles becoming more natural.

"Jared has a big day planned for you, so I won't keep you any longer." His mom included both Sharon and Jared in her smile. Her green eyes twinkled, and he sensed her approval. She looked from Mindy to Kitty and crouched down, her hands on the knees of her slacks. "And when you get back, we'll have a real Vermont treat. Ever hear of sugar on snow?"

Both girls shook their heads, their eyes wide, and his mom chuckled.

"You will."

thirteen

Once Sharon had gotten over the initial shock of Jared's family "farm" and how massive it really was, she allowed herself to relax. His family put her at ease with their friendly smiles and conversation, treating her and her kids as if they'd always belonged to the family. At first she found that a bit strange; most folks in Goosebury showed a reserve toward newcomers, and it often took time to work toward acceptance. Sharon wondered if the Crisp family treated everyone with such friendly welcome, or if Jared had told them so much about her they felt like they knew her.

That thought brought heat to her cheeks, welcome in the cold, crisp air as Jared took them along the thickly wooded trail.

"This is my trail," he told the girls. "Every afternoon I collect tree sap from the buckets." He pointed to several sugar maples, huge in diameter, with two taps instead of just one.

With a few well-aimed words to garner Andy's interest, Jared let her son take a few turns at carrying the buckets and dumping the sap inside the barrel at the back of the wagon. Of course, Kitty and Mindy then insisted they have a turn, and Jared had little choice but to allow it—that or hear their constant pleadings. Sharon watched him lower the bucket suspended from the hook of the spout and place it into Mindy's hands, instructing her to carry it to the wagon. He then hoisted her up so she could pour it into the barrel.

"There sure are lots of trees," Mindy said as Jared rehung the bucket from the spout. "Do you have to get the sap from all of them every day?"

"Yup. Every day. Me and my family. There's too much here for one person to do, though we don't have to worry about the trees on the hills. They have tubing that takes the sap right to the tank." He pointed to the nearest hill, and the kids stared, openmouthed.

"Dad assigned trails to us when we started helping with the gathering," Jared said. "For the next three to six weeks, depending on the weather, I'll collect the sap from buckets on my route so those working in the sugarhouse can boil it to make maple syrup. We start the process after a few sunny days when it gets warm—in the forties—but the nights are still freezing. That's the best time for the sap to flow."

Kitty peered into the bucket Jared had just positioned. "Look, more is starting to drip out of the tree," she said. "But it's so slow."

"A tree that size, from one tap, will yield about fifteen gallons of sap a year. It takes almost ten gallons to produce one quart of maple syrup—the size of the jugs we sell."

"Wow," Andy said under his breath. "That's a lot of sap."

Andy's interest in Jared's informative words cheered Sharon. Since Jared had picked them up at the house, Andy hadn't shown animosity toward him, and Sharon hoped those days were over. She had seen a change in his attitude since he'd started working at Hugh's farm, though she still didn't feel comfortable with his attachment to the moose calf, which had strengthened through the months.

As the horse-drawn sleigh whisked over the crisp snow, still deep for early March, the sun beamed down from high above, making the snow on the limbs glitter like diamonds in a crystalline world.

Once they collected all the sap, Jared took them to the sugarhouse to watch the sugaring process. Inside the warm room, the sweet smell of maple sugar permeated the air.

First he showed them an evaporator, a machine that stood a few inches under Jared's height and three times as wide. He introduced them to the man who worked it, his brother-in-law, Greg.

Kitty edged closer to try to get a better look, and Sharon called her back before she hurt herself. She had seen the quantities of steam billow from the chimneys before they'd entered the building.

"They use a very hot fire to dissolve the water from the sap," Jared explained as if reading Sharon's mind. "That's what this machine does. The sap has to be boiled right away, or it begins to spoil. I'll let Greg tell you more." He slapped his brother-in-law on the shoulder.

The three children as well as Sharon listened to Greg's detailed explanation of what happened to the sap in the evaporator as it took a winding path along different pans, becoming denser with the process. He then introduced them to another man, who showed them the hydrometer, where the sap was checked for proper density, then passed along to a pump which filtered out what he called sugar sand. The result was a fine golden syrup he called "liquid gold." This they stored in a steel drum until ready to be packaged in small containers for distribution.

"Wow, all that just to make syrup," Mindy said in awe.

Sharon noted the rapt expressions on her children's faces. Even Andy appeared intrigued, and she was glad she'd agreed to come. She had enjoyed the tour so far, more so because Jared led it. The past months without him had been difficult, and she'd reached the point of admitting she needed his presence in their lives.

Next Jared took them to the confectionary kitchen, where three women were hard at work. He moved to a dark-haired young woman who stood at the end of a counter and gave her a one-armed hug as he looked into the huge, stainless steel bowl she stirred. "What are you making?"

She shook her head and rolled her eyes with a smile. "You know exactly what I'm making, and yes, you can have some." She spooned a bit of the close-to-a-peanut-butter-consistency spread off onto another spoon and from there onto her finger, slipping it into his mouth.

"Jared's always loved maple cream," she explained to Sharon, who had watched, wide-eyed, the whole exchange with the mystery woman. "Ever since he was a tot running around in diapers."

"Thank you so much for that informative comment, Amy," he drawled. "Sharon, my sister, Amy. The oldest of my siblings, but by no means the wisest." She swatted his arm, and he pulled away in mock pain, grinning all the while.

"It is so nice to meet you," Amy said, her brown eyes alight with friendliness. "When Jared was born," she explained to Sharon, "he was the first boy, and Alice, Andrea, and I spoiled him rotten. Oh, fools that we mortals be." She looked up at the ceiling as if addressing the heavens, and Jared gave her hair a gentle yank.

"You love me, and you know it," he shot back.

"Ah, yes," she said in mock despair. "Like I said—fools and mortals."

Enjoying their banter, Sharon smiled with relief to learn they were siblings.

"And these are my cousins." He continued the introduction as he smiled at two young blonds. "Emily and Grace."

The women nodded shy hellos, which Sharon returned. Using fancy-shaped leaf molds, both women cut candy. At Jared's nod, they offered a sample piece to each of the children, who grabbed the sweets up from the platter with eager thanks.

"This entire farm really is all family operated, isn't it?" Sharon asked, thinking of all the cousins, brothers, and sisters she'd met. "When your aunts said all of the family takes part in some way, they weren't joking."

Jared laughed. "Yup, just about everyone has a hand at the Sugarwoods, though a few, like Becca, have become traitors and work outside the farm," he joked. "To be fair, she takes a hand with the tourists once in a while, especially helping out at the petting zoo."

"Petting zoo?" Kitty asked, her eyes wide.

"We open it in April. You'll have to come back then," he added and looked Sharon's way. Her heart gave a little jump at the idea of returning. What had been a frightening prospect now appealed.

"For the most part, it's all family here," Jared continued from where he'd left off. "My dad has ten brothers and sisters, so when you figure out the generations, that does amount to a lot of workers. Even the small kids have chores to help out."

"Does all of your family live on the land?" Sharon asked in shock.

"Not all of them, no. Most of those who do have their own places."

"It's like your own little community," she mused.

"I suppose so. My grandfather left an equal share in the farm to each of his sons and daughters, and smaller shares to us grandkids. We all have a part in its operation and in voicing opinions during family meetings. Case in point, we recently voted in favor of a reverse osmosis machine that will help speed up the evaporation process. We still stick to old-fashioned ideas and methods but have allowed room for more modern technology in some areas.

"Would you like to see the Crisp farmhouse store and the items we sell?" he asked the girls.

"Sure!" Mindy responded.

The small tourist shop, with its bottles, jars, and tubs of

maple syrups, creams, and candies was inviting. A few tourists stood at the back of the store, trying to decide between two packaged gift sets. Sharon recognized products that Jared's aunts sold in their souvenir-craft store, as well.

Jared's cousin behind the counter seemed as nice as the rest of the Crisp clan, though she watched Sharon the entire time with curious interest. Sharon had begun to see a pattern. At the mention of her name upon Jared's introduction, many looked at Sharon with recognition, and she recalled Jared once told her he'd spoken about her—but she didn't realize he meant to his entire family! She wasn't sure how she felt about that. He'd been quite verbal about his interest in her when they'd met last summer, and these past months without him had given her a lot of time to think. Even before discovering the Bible instruction to young widows to marry was true, Sharon realized she'd lost her heart to Jared long ago.

Counseling with the pastor's wife and some heart-to-heart talks with Leslie had helped Sharon reach a new stepping-stone in her bridge to healing. She no longer allowed old, painful memories from years before to pull her away from the desire for Jared's touch. Now she anticipated it, though she had no idea how to tell him so. Still, despite these new feelings, she didn't know if she was ready for more.

"You guys want to celebrate a springtime sugaring tradition?" Jared asked.

The girls answered with eager squeals, and they returned to the farmhouse where his mom, sister, and nieces greeted them with smiles. Three boys and girls also joined them, and Sharon learned they were Amy's kids.

His mom led the troupe to a huge kitchen, where Jared, Sharon, and the children sat around the large table. His mom heated a pot of syrup, using a candy thermometer. After a few minutes, she nodded to Jared. He grabbed an empty pan and went outside, grinning mysteriously. The children and Sharon looked at the Crisp women puzzled, but only more mysterious smiles greeted them. Jared's sister Alice set out a bowl of dill pickles, and his teenage nieces, Tamara and Beth, poured coffee and put out yeast doughnuts. Jared returned minutes later, the pan full of snow.

"Why'd you bring snow inside?" Kitty wanted to know. "Won't it melt?"

"Watch, and you'll see." He set the pan on the table and scooped snow into individual containers Alice set out. His mom brought the hot syrup from the stove and drizzled a light helping onto each mound of pure white snow. The children's eyes grew wide as the maple syrup formed lace-like patterns across the top of the snow and quickly hardened. His mom handed a container and fork to each of them. The children wasted no time in sampling the sweet.

"Mmmm," Kitty said. "This is better than a candy factory!"

"What do you mean?" Mindy asked as she bit into her own golden-brown serving. "This *is* a candy factory!"

Many of them laughed along with the girls, who began to sing the "Toot Sweets" song from the *Chitty Chitty Bang Bang* movie they'd seen the previous year, broken up by a good deal of giggling from Kitty as she tried to whistle through the candy.

"Silly girl." Caught up in the fun, Sharon wrapped her arms around Kitty, who sat beside her, and sprinkled her cheek with kisses.

"Stop it, Mama," Kitty laughingly protested. "They're all sweet and sugared!"

"Well, darling," Jared's mom said with a smile, "that's what love is. Sweet as sugar."

Without meaning to, Sharon's gaze met and locked with Jared's across the table. His eyes held a wealth of emotion, though his face remained blank. A strange, sort of hopeful expectation cornered her thoughts, and warmth suffused her face before she tore her gaze away from his and tried to concentrate on her treat.

"Now eat a bite of pickle," Jared's mom suggested to the girls.

"A pickle?" Kitty's nose wrinkled. "Yuk."

"Try it," Alice urged. "It's really good. It takes the edge off the sweetness. Doughnuts are good with it, too."

Sharon had to agree as she forked some of the extremely sweet taffy like candy into her mouth and followed it with a bite of juicy dill pickle. Andy wolfed his down in no time and asked for seconds. Sharon would have corrected him, but Jared's mom already held the ladle poised over the snow, and Billy, Amy's son who was around Andy's age, also held his bowl out for more.

The group broke up after a relaxing time of conversation while they all enjoyed their treats. Amy's girls asked Mindy and Kitty to join them in playing a board game, and Billy asked Andy if he wanted to see his CD collection. Sharon nodded for her kids to go ahead. A few minutes of conversation ensued among the adults before Jared turned to Sharon. "Would you like to take a walk?"

Sharon's heart leaped at the prospect of spending time alone with him, after her recent thoughts, but she nodded. Thanking the rest of the Crisp family, she walked with him out the back kitchen door that led to the mudroom, and from there, outside.

ॐ

Jared walked with Sharon across the snowy yard. He wondered if he imagined the hope in her eyes when his mom talked of love, but now that they were alone for the first time in months, he didn't want to scare her away by asking.

"How have you been?" He glanced her way.

"Good. Andy had a birthday last month, so now I'm the mother of a teenager."

"That's hard to believe," he said admiring her youthful face. "You don't look a day over twenty-one."

She laughed. "Sometimes I feel twice that. Having kids is great, but they can wear a person down."

"Single parenthood must be tough."

"It can be."

Their words held a host of unspoken thoughts regarding their situation, and a moment of awkwardness passed between them.

"I guess you heard about Kim?" she asked after a minute.

"The girl from church?"

"Yes."

"I've been busy at the farm and am behind on current events. What about Kim?"

"She had surgery in January. Her sight was restored."

"That's terrific! You don't seem happy." He noted the lines between her brows. Jared led her through a patch of trees, pushing a low twiggy branch aside and clearing the way for her to pass.

"Oh, I am. I'm thrilled for Kim. But Carly told me just a few weeks after the operation Kim started having problems. When the doctor examined her, he said there's a chance she might go blind again; that these results won't last."

"That's hard." Jared felt a twinge of sympathy for the brave teenager.

"Chris is more upset than most—Chris is the guy she's been dating, Nate's cousin. He asked her to marry him after he graduates from college in a few years, but she refused and broke up with him. Carly said it's because she's afraid she'll go blind again and doesn't want to be a burden to Chris. Which is ridiculous, since he's loved Kim from the day they met—and she was blind then."

"One-sided love can be a tough situation. I understand his pain."

At his telling words, she stopped and looked at him sharply. "Oh, she loves him; she's just scared and isn't thinking straight right now."

"And I'm sure he's just as scared. Of losing her." He stared into her eyes, his expression as intent as hers. "Especially since she told him to leave, and she's run from him, closing him out."

"She can't help the way she feels. She's been through a lot."

"I understand that, but she has to come to a place where she realizes she doesn't need to go through those feelings alone."

"She's a private person, afraid to open up."

"But she won't be happy until she allows love back into her life and allows herself to love again. He's there for her and wants to grow old with her, to share a life with her and her kids."

"Her kids," Sharon whispered. "Who are we talking about here, Jared?"

He withheld an answer, but he saw the knowledge in her eyes, the affirmation that they had been discussing the same thing.

"I'm afraid."

"I know."

"Not of you." She gave a slight shake of her head.

"I know that, too." He lifted his hands to cradle either side of her head, his eyes searching hers.

She blinked up at him, but no fear touched her expression, only an uncertain hope. She glanced down at his mouth and moistened her lower lip.

All restraint dissolved when he realized she hadn't pulled away, had, in fact, swayed closer.

He lowered his head and brushed his lips against her soft ones. Slow, gentle. More than once. His heart felt as if it might race out of his body, and his breathing grew unsteady. He didn't deepen the kiss, though he wanted to. Instead, he lifted his head to look at her.

She opened her eyes as if awakening after a long sleep, her own chest rising and falling faster than before. They stared at one another a long moment.

Like a woman coming out of a trance, she lifted her fingertips to touch his lips, her gaze on his mouth.

He took her hand in his and dropped a gentle kiss on her fingers, before lowering it so he could speak. "Sharon, I love you. I want to spend my life with you."

"I don't know if I can give you that." She looked up at him, her eyes vulnerable and concerned. "I might end up disappointing you, and I don't want to. I just don't know if I can marry again."

"We don't have to jump into anything. Let's just take this one step at a time."

She hesitated. "Why did you stay away so long? Why didn't you call before today?"

Her quiet words gave him hope. "If I could have come earlier, I would have. Funny thing, my brother suggested I stay away to give you space; I didn't intend to though. Things have been so busy here. Though to be honest, with the way you ran out of church after the Christmas program, I didn't think you'd mind the break away from me."

"I did mind." She lowered her eyes, her lashes fanning her cheeks. "I missed you."

Her admission made Jared want to kiss her again, but he refrained.

"I want to show you something."

"What?" she looked confused at the change of topic.

"You'll see."

He kept her hand in his as they spent the next five minutes

walking through the trees to the other side, sharing glances now and then.

She exhaled, startled, as they reached a small clearing. "Is this your cabin?" she asked, looking with approval at the log building against a backdrop of trees. At his nod, she went on, "It's so cozy." She studied the entire area. Through a clearing, the distant Green Mountains rose in gentle slopes. "And so peaceful," she breathed.

"In the evenings, you can see the sun set over the mountains." Intent on her reaction, he watched her.

"It's beautiful here, Jared. Thank you for showing me your home."

He had wanted to show her this spot for months. "My grandparents left me this plot of land, from beyond those trees"—he motioned with his arm in the distance—"to over there, where those two white pines stand close together. I own the cabin, too. Remember when I joked with you at the mall and said I thought I might go into construction when I was younger?"

His revelations made her eyes go wide. "Yes," she whispered.

"Well, I had a hand in building this cabin. I always thought some day I might add on to it, if the need ever arose." He left his meaning unsaid but saw by her dazed nod that she understood. And by her averted gaze, he knew when to stop.

He held out his hand to her. "One step at a time, Sharon. That's all I ask."

She nodded, her eyes alight with hope, and took his hand. Together they walked back to the farmhouse.

fourteen

Months later, Sharon paced the den, about to go out of her mind. At the sound of a knock, she hurried to open the door and pulled Jared inside, out of the early morning darkness.

He drew her close, and she melted against him, taking comfort in his strong arms. "I don't know what to do," she said against his shirt, trying not to fall apart.

He cupped the back of her head and smoothed his hand down her hair. "Tell me what happened."

"Yesterday Hugh told us he's selling the farm; he's retiring as a wildlife rehabilitator, too." She tried to calm down. "That was bad enough, but then Andy and I argued about bringing the moose here—I told you her leg got wounded somehow a week ago and Hugh's been taking care of it?"

"Yes."

"Well, Andy hasn't been happy with me about any of that. . .and other things." She sighed. Ever since she and Jared had started seeing each other on a more personal level, she and Andy had butted heads.

"We had something of a shouting fest. He ended up locking himself in his room. I had a bad dream and couldn't get back to sleep. So I got up and found Andy had gone. His backpack is missing, and a carton of pudding cups is gone, too." She realized in her panic, her words rambled. "Kitty's still too sick with the flu to leave her alone, and I don't know what to do."

"Did you call the police?"

"No, only you."

He held her from him, his hands clasping her shoulders.

152

"I'll find him, Sharon. It's going to be all right."

The strength of his words and sincerity in his eyes helped her believe him, and she nodded. His smile encouraging, he bent to deposit a gentle kiss to her lips before retracing his steps out the front door.

Anxious, Sharon stood in the entrance, hugging herself, bereft of Jared's consoling warmth and fearful for her son's safety. She watched Jared pull a flashlight from his glove compartment. He beamed the glow onto the pavement while striding toward the lane, then turned and saw her standing in the doorway.

"He walked through the lawn and tracked mud down the drive," Jared called as he moved to his car. "His footprints lead south. I'll drive that way; he couldn't have gotten far."

Sharon nodded, though she doubted he saw her. She watched his headlights cut through darkness as he reversed and swung the car south along the road.

"Mama?"

At the sound of Kitty's weak voice, Sharon closed the door against the chill and turned to her youngest daughter.

Kitty's eyes still shone fever-bright, and she trembled in her bed gown, her feet bare on the cold floor.

"What's wrong, Kitty?" Sharon approached and knelt before her. Out of habit, she pressed her forearm to Kitty's brow to check her temperature and found it still flame hot. "You should be in bed, honey."

"Did Andy run away?" Her voice grated hoarse from a sore throat.

"Andy'll be fine," Sharon reassured, smoothing her hand down her daughter's hair, much as Jared had done with her. Sharon put her hand to Kitty's shoulder, pushing her daughter back along the lit hallway and into her darkened room.

"Was Jared here?" Kitty asked as she crawled into her bed

and Sharon pulled the covers up over her. Mindy lay sound asleep in the next bed.

"Yes, he came over for a little while." Sharon didn't want to worry her daughter.

"It'll be okay, Mama," Kitty said, her eyes drowsy. "Jared will find Andy. He always helps us."

Sharon stared with amazement at her youngest child. She wished she possessed even half of Kitty's unwavering and unconditional trust, the ability to accept another's words without question. But a lifetime of hurt had drained trust from Sharon with slow persistence.

Two weeks before, Jared had officially proposed. In the months they'd grown closer, Sharon had wanted to spend every moment with him, but her fear to trust in full held her back from giving him the answer he desired. She'd been blind when they first met, blind to what an incredible man Jared was, and later, blind to her feelings regarding him. Since then, she'd opened her eyes to the truth and accepted the knowledge that she loved him, but she couldn't fight the persistent niggling of doubt that to marry again, to entrust her life to another man, could be a mistake. Even to a man as wonderful and kind and patient as Jared. Her mind's logic argued the point while her heart's vulnerability embraced the idea of a lifetime with him, of having children with him. If only she could get her head and her heart to agree.

❧

Tense, Jared drove the car slowly down the lane, his foot barely touching the pedal as he watched for signs of movement on both sides of the road. About four miles farther, he exhaled a sigh of relief when his headlights caught Andy's hunched figure. The boy trudged along with his hands in his jacket pockets. Jared could tell he was tired.

Slowing the car to a crawl, he rolled down the automatic

window on the passenger side. Andy looked over, as if hope
ful for a ride, and Jared prayed the boy hadn't considered
hitchhiking. When he saw Jared, Andy frowned.

"What do you want?" he asked, his breath coming fast.

"Ten miles is a long walk," Jared replied, realizing it best to
proceed with caution.

Andy's expression registered surprise that Jared would figure
out where he was headed.

"Yeah, well, I can handle it."

Jared inched the car forward next to Andy while the boy
stomped onward.

"Hugh installed one of the best security systems on his farm
last year. Did he tell you? A burglar broke in last summer and
took off with some expensive equipment." Andy kept walking,
ignoring Jared. "Even if you make it there without keeling
over, you won't get far, Andy. The police will be there before
you can get to the moose, and then they'll have to take you to
jail and call your mom. You don't want to put her through all
that, do you?"

"What do you care?" He stopped walking and turned on
Jared.

"She's frantic now," Jared replied, keeping his tone calm.
"Why not get in, and I'll take you home? You two can talk
about it there."

"I don't need you to tell me what to do!"

"Well, the road you're headed down will only make you
more exhausted than you probably already are, and you'll wind
up in jail besides."

The boy seemed about to argue, then, to Jared's surprise,
wrenched open the door and ducked inside.

Andy remained quiet on the return drive, and when they
pulled up the lane, he hauled out of the car before Jared could
say a word. Instead of entering the front door, where Sharon

appeared, the boy ran to the barn.

Now what's he up to?

Jared turned off the car and got out. "I'll handle it," he quietly called to Sharon, whose face seemed a mask of distressed confusion.

She hesitated, then nodded and closed the door.

The moment he entered the barn, Jared spotted Andy. The boy sat with his shoes flat on the ground, his back against the wall in the same corner the moose had inhabited.

Jared stood just inside, leaving the door ajar so the moon gave them some light. Under the circumstances, he debated whether or not he ought to speak.

"I know it's hard to let go of something you care about," he said at last. "But you want the moose happy; Hugh's a trained professional and wants the best for her, too. He's not going to let her go before she's ready to survive in the wild."

The boy scowled, remaining silent.

"Even if the law allowed you to keep Caramel, she wouldn't be happy here. And I doubt you would be happy seeing her unhappy." Jared gave a cursory glance around the cramped barn. "She's not a moose calf anymore. She's a yearling—almost her full size now—and she needs the wide outdoors to run and play and roam. She needs to be around others of her own kind."

"What do you know?" Andy yelled, tears shining in his eyes. "She got hurt once already. She's not safe out in the wild. There are predators and hunters and other people who can hurt her. She needs me! I have to protect her."

"What happened to her was a fluke, Andy. Hugh said it looked as if she got stuck in some barbed wire. I'm sure she'll be fine."

"No, she won't! She doesn't know what mean people there are out there. But I do. Men who can hurt her and kick her and hit her, again and again and again. . . ." As he spoke, he struck his fist against his palm, each smack harder and bringing with it more tears, until he was sobbing. "She needs me to protect her. I have to save her. . . ."

Stunned by Andy's behavior, Jared felt out of his depth as he realized they were talking about more than the moose.

"Andy," he said, trying to sound reassuring, calm. "Little boys can't be expected to stop big, strong men from hurting the people they love."

The boy looked up at him sharply.

Jared took a chance, hoping it wasn't a mistake. "No one blames you, least of all your mom. It wasn't your place to protect her. Children aren't meant to protect their parents; it's supposed to be the other way around."

"What do you know about any of it?"

"I don't. But I do know your mom has let go of the past and, in doing so, found peace. She trusts God to protect her now."

"Will He protect her from *you*?" Andy sneered.

Jared regarded him with surprise. "From me?"

"Yeah, I'll bet you want to marry her just so you can start beating up on her like my dad did!"

Faced again with the horror of what Sharon had gone through, Jared winced. "Andy, I love your mother. Marriage is about sharing love and trust and being committed to doing all you possibly can to help one another. It isn't about creating violence and hate." He realized from what Sharon had told him that her stepfather had done the same to her mother. No wonder the boy resented Sharon's relationship with Jared and despised him! He'd witnessed abuse in marriages all of his young life.

"What happened to your mom isn't how marriage is supposed to be, Andy. God intended for two people—a man and his wife—to become one. To be a team, but more than that, to love and care for one another, to offer each other support.

Hatred only divides and tears down. Some men. . ." He trod with caution, not wanting to squash any feelings Andy may have for his dad. "Some men never understand what a real marriage is. Their selfish desires or wrong ideas they've learned cloud the issue. I only want the absolute best for your mom—she deserves all the happiness she can get. All of you do. And if I thought making her happy meant that I should leave you guys alone, I'd do it. Even though it would hurt me to let her go. Letting go hurts. But if you really care about something, like you do your moose, or love someone, like I do your mom, then you want what's best for them. You don't want them to live in cages—forced into an existence that you want so you can be near them. You want them to live the life they were meant to live, that God meant them to have. The life that will make them happiest."

The boy remained quiet, and Jared wondered if he'd even been listening.

"You'd really go away if you thought that would make Mom happy?" he asked, his eyes watchful.

Jared sighed and nodded, not surprised that of all he'd said, Andy would latch onto that. "If I thought your mom would be happier without me, I'd leave right now. I never want to see her hurt and never would do anything to hurt her. When she hurts, I hurt." Jared took it a step further. "My dad raised me to respect women, to protect them and help them if they need it. Women are supposed to be cherished. God highly favored them; He gave them the gift to produce life and bear children."

Silence, thick and heavy, stretched between them. Andy stared at his shoes, and Jared wished he could see his expression. He wished Andy would speak, felt the desire to urge him to, but at the same time dared not force him.

"She cried," Andy broke the endless span of silence.

"What?" Taken aback by the sudden words and surprising switch of topic, Jared peered at the boy. His scowl had disappeared; his manner was resigned.

"Mom. She cried when you quit coming around after Christmas. She didn't know I heard her in her room, but it was because she missed you."

⮿

Sharon had walked to the barn earlier, but upon hearing Jared speak to her son, she remained outside, loath to interfere yet unable to leave. She leaned against the barn's doorjamb, feeling her son's pain, but she knew he needed to hear Jared out before she stepped forward. At Andy's admission of her feelings for Jared, she clapped her hand over her mouth while tears rushed to her eyes.

She thought she'd fooled everyone by her apparent indifference, but she'd ended up fooling only herself. Through the lesson of the moose, Jared had reached Andy in a way Sharon never had, and Andy had opened up to him. Jared's sincere explanation of marriage and his admission of his love for her warmed Sharon's heart to overflowing. She didn't want to live another day without such a man. She desired to spend each year with him, working beside him on his farm, living in his cabin, raising their children, both the ones she now had and the ones she hoped to give him.

She was weary of being single, weary of living in a web of doubt related to the past, a past that she'd long ago put behind her. In the year she'd known him, Jared had shown that he deserved her trust. He loved her, loved her kids, and his actions proved it.

Unable to prevent herself, she entered the barn. Jared turned in surprise, his curious expression changing to awe as their eyes met and held and he read the message she felt sure must beam from her face in the moon's glow.

Andy stood up. Sharon sensed him glancing from her to Jared, before moving forward. His arms went around her shoulders in a strong hug, and she looked at him in surprise. A pang went through her to realize how tall he'd grown this past month alone; he possessed the husky build of a young man and stood almost as tall as she did now.

"I'm sorry I was such a pain, Mom," he said, a catch in his voice, which also had begun to crack with the disappearance of childhood. "I don't mean to be."

"You're not a pain, son. I just want you to be happy. I want that for all my children, and when I can't give them what they need or want, it hurts. I'm sorry about Caramel, believe me."

"I understand about the moose," he said quiet, bowing his head. "I really don't want Caramel living in a dark barn that's too small for her. I want her to be happy in the wild. But is it all right if we visit her tomorrow before Mr. MacFarland sets her free again? Even though it's a weekday?"

Sharon hesitated.

"I just want to say good-bye. I won't do nothin' wrong. Honest."

"Okay." She hugged him close, rubbing her hand up and down his arm.

"And maybe, sometime, can we get a dog?"

Sharon laughed. "I think that would be a great idea, Andy."

"As a matter of fact," Jared said, "one of the collies on the farm had pups this spring. How would you like first pick of the litter?"

"Cool." Andy smiled for the first time that night. "I like collies."

Sharon glanced up at Jared in gratitude, and again their eyes held.

"Well," Andy said, sticking his hands in his jacket pockets, and looking back and forth between the two, "I guess I'll head back to the house. I'm sure you guys want to talk about all that sweet, sugared stuff."

Sharon glanced at him in surprise, realizing by his words, he finally approved.

"Don't stay out too long, Mom," he said with a cheeky grin. "It's way past your bedtime."

Andy left, and Sharon shook her head. "I guess he'll always be protective, but I wasn't expecting that!" The same startled amusement was apparent on Jared's face.

"He's growing up," Jared said. "It's good for him to hold on to those protective qualities, since it's all part of learning to be a man, as long as he doesn't let it interfere with his being a kid."

She regarded him, her smile tender, and he walked close, his expression just as soft.

"About what he said, is that what you wanted to talk about?" His brow lifted. "The sweet sugared stuff?"

For an answer, she pressed her hands to his waist and lifted herself on her toes to kiss him. She saw the surprise in his eyes when she pulled back.

"What was that for?"

"To thank you for being you, for your help with Andy. . ."

He raised his brow as her words trailed off, unfinished.

She took a breath. "And to let you know I'm ready to take that final step."

As her comment sunk in, his eyes grew a little bigger. "You mean. . . ?"

"Yes, Jared, I want to marry you."

He threw his arms around her and picked her up off the ground. She squealed, laughing, as he spun around with her one time, and linking her wrists behind his neck, she lowered her head and kissed him.

❧

A month later, Sharon stood in a room at the back of the

church, adjusting her short veil over her head. Neither she nor Jared had wanted a long engagement, both of them certain this was the road they wanted and should take. No more doubts had visited Sharon since the night she'd agreed to marry Jared; if anything, every day brought further confirmation that this was God's plan for a new future. A better future.

Denied a wedding dress for her first wedding, which had been a quick ceremony in front of the justice of the peace, Sharon defied tradition for a previously married woman and wore an ice-white, ankle-length, wedding gown covered in tiny flower-patterns of crystals along a round neckline.

"I can't believe you made that," Carly said, fluffing Sharon's dress as she looked at the crown that held Sharon's veil. "You have loads of talent, Angel."

Sharon smiled, wondering if Jared would think her sentimental action silly. She'd taken the Dollar-Store tiara he'd bought during last year's Christmas shopping excursion, his first gift to her, and with lengths of gauze and fancy cording, created a veil that matched the gown in a way that didn't look gaudy, but professionally made. Not only had she broken tradition by wearing white for a second wedding, but also she'd chosen to do something else out of the ordinary. A surprise, and her wedding gift to Jared.

"I hope I don't let you down," Leslie said. "It's been a long time since I played, back when I was living with my mother."

"Don't worry, Leslie, you'll do fine." Sharon had asked Jill to be her organist, but her tiny daughter, Lila, had decided to make an appearance into the world the day before—a month and a half early. Jared had promised Sharon that before they left for their honeymoon in Cancun, they would drop in to visit Jill and her new daughter, both of whom were doing well.

"Are you ready?" Leslie asked Sharon.

She nodded, thinking it ironic that her friends seemed more nervous than she was.

As she took her short and long-awaited journey down the aisle, she noticed Kim at the back, sitting beside Chris, both of them smiling, their arms linked through one another's as they held hands. Chris had never given up on Kim and finally convinced her that he wasn't going anywhere and would always love her, come what may. Whether she went blind again or not, he'd made it clear he wanted always to be a part of her life.

Jared had done much the same with Sharon; from the start he'd been there for her when she needed him. Sharon loved and trusted him, though she knew he was fallible and didn't always make the right decisions—like in staying absent this past winter and not calling her, no matter that he had a viable excuse; she really must teach him how to use a phone.

Life had no guarantees; troubles came, bad things happened. But she'd reached the knowledge that she couldn't hide from a personal future, fearing its outcome. Instead she must trust God. He would never let her down. The Lord had confirmed to Sharon that marrying Jared was His will; He'd just confirmed it for Jared a great deal faster. She grinned with fond remembrance when she thought about their first meeting, when Jared had blurted out that she was his future wife and she'd thought him a crackpot. Now here she was, joining him at the altar to unite with him for the rest of their lives.

Her three kids sat beside her mother in the front pew. Even her stepfather had come, and Sharon had to admit she'd noticed a change in his behavior; she only prayed it would last. Her mother had read the book and just the other night had asked Sharon questions about God; a good sign. Sharon could only hope and pray her mother's interest would continue.

Looking like fairy-tale princesses in their long, pastel dresses, their blond hair perfectly styled, Mindy and Kitty appeared as if they might start bouncing up and down in the pew from barely contained excitement, and she winked at them. In his black suit, Andy looked like a young man. Sharon felt a catch in her throat at how fast her son was growing up. He had released his animosity toward Jared, though their relationship was still a bit rocky at times. But Andy was coming along, and for that Sharon felt gratitude.

Every pew on Jared's side of the church was filled, half of them by family alone. And now his family was her family.

As she took her place beside Jared, she smiled, her heart beating fast at the awe and love in his eyes. She'd never seen him in formal attire; he looked so handsome. The ceremony commenced, and the time arrived to present her gift to him. Her palms moist, she brushed her fingertips across them, keeping her hands down at her sides.

Leslie played the organ while Sharon faced Jared and sang for him the vow of love she'd written, to express all he meant to her. He watched, amazed, the delight on his face evident. Before today, she'd never sung for him. Before today, she had never felt she could.

Once they exchanged vows, once Pastor Neil pronounced them husband and wife and they kissed to seal their promise to one another, Jared linked her arm through his and covered her hand with his own. They smiled at one another, then retraced their steps up the aisle and to the back of the church while pleased family and friends looked on.

Outside the church doors, Jared drew Sharon close for a rare moment of privacy before the guests could congregate around them with congratulations and well wishes.

"My princess—you look like a princess today." His expression was tender. "And at last, my wife. You're one gorgeous woman, Sharon."

"You recognize the crown?" she asked, a bit shy at his praise.

Taken aback, he glanced at the top of her veil. "That's the same one I bought you last Christmas? You made that?"

She nodded.

He shook his head in wonder. "You're amazing; God's blessed you with so many talents, and the voice of an angel besides. No wonder Carly calls you Angel. I never knew you could sing like that."

No condemnation traced his voice, only curiosity.

"For a long time, I haven't been able to sing. I didn't even want to. The sorrow of the past few years sucked the desire right out of me. But you gave music back to me, Jared. You replaced that spark of life and resurrected old desires, and not just the singing. You've helped me to rediscover *life*."

His fingertips traced her cheek. "Now we have our entire life before us, to discover together."

She nodded with a smile, and as they shared one last tender kiss before the guests' arrival, she anticipated learning the future with him.

epilogue

Two-and-a-half years later

Arm in arm, Jared and Sharon strolled through the vast acreage of the Sugarwoods. Ahead of them, Mindy and Kitty sang as they skipped, jogged, and ran—walking was not in their vocabulary. Andy held a branch, which he tapped on tree trunks as he passed them, and Sharon winced when she remembered his latest declaration that he wanted to be a drummer.

Now that both she and Jared taught the children's choir at their church, she supposed it shouldn't surprise her that her son's interest had gravitated to music, but the thought of banging and cymbals all hours of the day didn't appeal. Still, in Andy's basement room, perhaps the noise wouldn't be too deafening, and Jared did assure Sharon he could soundproof the room.

Sharon had quit her job at A'bric & A'brac not long after she and Jared married, and she'd been working alongside the Crisp family ever since while learning about life on a sugar maple farm. She loved it. Often she accompanied Jared on his deliveries, and they stayed to dinner at his aunts'. In the spring, she helped make candy and enjoyed mingling with the tourist children at the petting zoo. She and Becca had become fast friends—she'd become friends with all of Jared's sisters, but she and Becca had known each other since the shared "day of the moose," and she felt closest to her.

With the impending snows, they enjoyed these lingering days of warm weather. As their walk continued, the girls ended their song, and Andy stopped slapping his stick against the trees. For a few brief minutes, Sharon treasured the silence of a Sunday afternoon, though she wished she could find a moment to speak alone with Jared.

They turned with the bend of the path and came into view of a cow moose and her calf about fifteen feet away. Jared's arm tightened around Sharon.

"Girls, move back toward us, nice and slow," he ordered, his voice tense but hushed. "Andy, you, too. No, don't turn around," he warned when Kitty started to pivot.

Terrified, Sharon stood still, wishing her children were far behind her. She knew how deadly a cow moose could become if she believed her calf endangered.

Andy stared at the moose a moment before he walked toward it. It lifted its head, its action abrupt.

"Andy! Stop, don't go any closer," Jared said.

"Dad, it's okay. It's my moose." Still, he did as Jared told him, and Sharon was grateful that Andy's rebellious days were in the past. Jared's loving but strong influence had brought her son in line like nothing else could.

"Caramel," Andy called. "Here, girl."

"Andy!" Sharon warned. "No."

The moose cow's ears went back, her eyes on Andy.

"Jared," Sharon whispered. "Do something!"

Kitty and Mindy had backed within reach. Jared moved Kitty behind him, and Sharon did the same with Mindy. Andy stood about ten feet ahead, too far for Sharon to grab without alerting the moose. Moose had bad eyesight, but she didn't know how bad and didn't want to make any sudden moves that might incite it to attack.

The moose snorted, tossing its head, and Sharon's adrenaline rocketed. "Jared," she pleaded under her breath.

" 'Amazing grace! How sweet the sound,' " Jared sang. Sharon glanced at him in shock. " 'That saved a wretch like me!' "

As he continued the verse, she joined him. Mindy's hand pressed against Sharon's back as she also began to sing; it gave her a strange comfort, the sense that all would be okay.

Her breath caught as the moose cow ambled toward them, its steps slow, wary. She watched, helpless and amazed, as the animal halted a foot from her son, and Andy stretched out his hand to its muzzle. Words of warning caught in her throat.

"Hey, Caramel," he said as if to a beloved pet. "How you doing, girl?"

She sensed Jared's amazement matched her own as they watched Andy's hand make contact with the moose's snout, then travel up along her head. She stood, quiet, and allowed him to stroke her.

"I don't believe this," Jared murmured in wonder.

Neither did Sharon. After such an extended time, she couldn't believe the moose would remember Andy. And obviously it was Andy's moose; the scar tissue from its tangle with the barbed wire on its front leg proved it.

For this miraculous window of time, God had not only protected one of His children; He'd allowed him to connect with one of His magnificent wild creatures in a manner Sharon doubted many people had before. No more than a few minutes passed before the moose nodded once, as if in farewell, and retraced its steps to the moose calf. Both animals walked out of sight and into the trees.

"She was thanking you, Andy," Kitty said, stepping from behind Jared, who stood as still and shocked as Sharon did. "For saving her and for taking care of her."

Jared smiled down at their daughter. "Maybe she was at that."

"And now she has a baby moose all her own to take care of," Kitty ended with a smile.

The soul-stirring moment left a sense of wonder behind,

a sense of the miraculous in the atmosphere. As Jared and Sharon held hands and retraced their steps, Sharon realized the perfect time had arrived. The children ran ahead, quieter but just as playful. Andy's voice teasing his sisters floated back to them.

"Jared?"

"Hmm?"

Sharon leaned up to whisper in his ear. "The moose isn't the only one with a baby to care for."

The shock on his face rivaled his reaction to the moose's interaction with Andy. Jared stopped on the path, swinging to face her.

"You're not. . . ?"

"I am." Her grin stretched wide. For two years they'd tried and failed. Early in the year, they at last came to a decision just to enjoy each other and the family God had already given them.

Jared shook his head, his eyes full of wonder, his mouth opening and closing but without words. He cradled her waist with extreme tenderness, as though afraid he might break her.

"You're okay?" he whispered.

"I'm fine."

"You're sure? I mean, about. . ."

Understanding his amazed disbelief, for it equaled what she'd felt when the doctor told her, she clasped his arms. "I had an appointment yesterday. I wanted to tell you as soon as I got home, but you were busy with the pipelines, and then when I finally got to bed last night after helping Mindy with her report, you were already asleep."

"I'm just so. . ." Moisture shone in his eyes. "God has taught me a huge lesson on the meaning of patience these past years and how, when I don't give in or give up, the promise is that much sweeter when it does come. But I'd thought we finally understood His answer about this." He shook his head, bemused. "I—I just can't believe it."

"God is full of surprises," Sharon agreed softly, so in love with her husband and with life.

"You sure you're feeling all right? Not too tired or anything? Maybe we should head back to the cabin or—"

Taking his face between her hands, she reached up and kissed him, cutting off his sweet concerns and showing him just how all right she truly was.

A Letter To Our Readers

Dear Reader:

In order that we might better contribute to your reading enjoyment, we would appreciate your taking a few minutes to respond to the following questions. We welcome your comments and read each form and letter we receive. When completed, please return to the following:

Fiction Editor
Heartsong Presents
PO Box 719
Uhrichsville, Ohio 44683

1. Did you enjoy reading *Sweet, Sugared Love* by Pamela Griffin?
   ❏ Very much! I would like to see more books by this author!
   ❏ Moderately. I would have enjoyed it more if

   _____

   _____

   _____

2. Are you a member of **Heartsong Presents**? ❏ Yes ❏ No
   If no, where did you purchase this book? _____

   _____

3. How would you rate, on a scale from 1 (poor) to 5 (superior), the cover design? _____

4. On a scale from 1 (poor) to 10 (superior), please rate the following elements.

   ____ Heroine   ____ Plot
   ____ Hero   ____ Inspirational theme
   ____ Setting   ____ Secondary characters

5. These characters were special because? _____

_____

_____

6. How has this book inspired your life? _____

_____

_____

7. What settings would you like to see covered in future
   Heartsong Presents books? _____

_____

_____

8. What are some inspirational themes you would like to see
   treated in future books? _____

_____

_____

9. Would you be interested in reading other **Heartsong
   Presents** titles? ❏ Yes ❏ No

10. Please check your age range:
    ❏ Under 18   ❏ 18-24
    ❏ 25-34   ❏ 35-45
    ❏ 46-55   ❏ Over 55

Name _____

Occupation _____

Address _____

City, State, Zip _____

Race to the Altar

4 stories in 1

*R*omance is in the air for NASCAR fans when couples meet as a result of their love for stock racing. Four stories by authors Ron Benrey, Gloria Clover, Becky Melby with Cathy Wienke, and Gail Sattler.

Contemporary, paperback, 352 pages, 5³/₁₆" x 8"

Please send me _____ copies of *Race to the Alter*. I am enclosing $6.97 for each. (Please add $3.00 to cover postage and handling per order. OH add 7% tax. If outside the U.S. please call 740-922-7280 for shipping charges.)

Name_____

Address _____

City, State, Zip _____

To place a credit card order, call 1-740-922-7280.
Send to: Heartsong Presents Readers' Service, PO Box 721, Uhrichsville, OH 44683

Heartng

CONTEMPORARY ROMANCE IS CHEAPER BY THE DOZEN!

Buy any assortment of twelve *Heartsong Presents* **titles and save 25% off the already discounted price of $2.97 each!**

Any 12 **Heartsong Presents** titles for only $27.00*

*plus $3.00 shipping and handling per order and sales tax where applicable. If outside the U.S. please call 740-922-7280 for shipping charges.

HEARTSONG PRESENTS TITLES AVAILABLE NOW:

___HP505 *Happily Ever After,* M. Panagiotopoulos
___HP506 *Cords of Love,* L. A. Coleman
___HP509 *His Christmas Angel,* G. Sattler
___HP510 *Past the Ps Please,* Y. Lehman
___HP513 *Licorice Kisses,* D. Mills
___HP514 *Roger's Return,* M. Davis
___HP517 *The Neighborly Thing to Do,* W. E. Brunstetter
___HP518 *For a Father's Love,* J. A. Grote
___HP521 *Be My Valentine,* J. Livingston
___HP522 *Angel's Roost,* J. Spaeth
___HP525 *Game of Pretend,* J. Odell
___HP526 *In Search of Love,* C. Lynxwiler
___HP529 *Major League Dad,* K. Y'Barbo
___HP530 *Joe's Diner,* G. Sattler
___HP533 *On a Clear Day,* Y. Lehman
___HP534 *Term of Love,* M. Pittman Crane
___HP537 *Close Enough to Perfect,* T. Fowler
___HP538 *A Storybook Finish,* L. Bliss
___HP541 *The Summer Girl,* A. Boeshaar
___HP542 *Clowning Around,* W. E. Brunstetter
___HP545 *Love Is Patient,* C. M. Hake
___HP546 *Love Is Kind,* J. Livingston
___HP549 *Patchwork and Politics,* C. Lynxwiler
___HP550 *Woodhaven Acres,* B. Etchison
___HP553 *Bay Island,* B. Loughner
___HP554 *A Donut a Day,* G. Sattler
___HP557 *If You Please,* T. Davis
___HP558 *A Fairy Tale Romance,* M. Panagiotopoulos
___HP561 *Ton's Vow,* K. Cornelius
___HP562 *Family Ties,* J. L. Barton
___HP565 *An Unbreakable Hope,* K. Billerbeck
___HP566 *The Baby Quilt,* J. Livingston
___HP569 *Ageless Love,* L. Bliss
___HP570 *Beguiling Masquerade,* C. G. Page
___HP573 *In a Land Far Far Away,* M. Panagiotopoulos

___HP574 *Lambert's Pride,* L. A. Coleman and R. Hauck
___HP577 *Anita's Fortune,* K. Cornelius
___HP578 *The Birthday Wish,* J. Livingston
___HP581 *Love Online,* K. Billerbeck
___HP582 *The Long Ride Home,* A. Boeshaar
___HP585 *Compassion's Charm,* D. Mills
___HP586 *A Single Rose,* P. Griffin
___HP589 *Changing Seasons,* C. Reece and J. Reece-Demarco
___HP590 *Secret Admirer,* G. Sattler
___HP593 *Angel Incognito,* J. Thompson
___HP594 *Out on a Limb,* G. Gaymer Martin
___HP597 *Let My Heart Go,* B. Huston
___HP598 *More Than Friends,* T. H. Murray
___HP601 *Timing is Everything,* T. V. Bateman
___HP602 *Dandelion Bride,* J. Livingston
___HP605 *Picture Imperfect,* N. J. Farrier
___HP606 *Mary's Choice,* Kay Cornelius
___HP609 *Through the Fire,* C. Lynxwiler
___HP610 *Going Home,* W. E. Brunstetter
___HP613 *Chorus of One,* J. Thompson
___HP614 *Forever in My Heart,* L. Ford
___HP617 *Run Fast, My Love,* P. Griffin
___HP618 *One Last Christmas,* J. Livingston
___HP621 *Forever Friends,* T. H. Murray
___HP622 *Time Will Tell,* L. Bliss
___HP625 *Love's Image,* D. Mayne
___HP626 *Down From the Cross,* J. Livingston
___HP629 *Look to the Heart,* T. Fowler
___HP630 *The Flat Marriage Fix,* K. Hayse
___HP633 *Longing for Home,* C. Lynxwiler
___HP634 *The Child Is Mine,* M. Colvin
___HP637 *Mother's Day,* J. Livingston
___HP638 *Real Treasure,* T. Davis
___HP641 *The Pastor's Assignment,* K. O'Brien
___HP642 *What's Cooking,* G. Sattler
___HP645 *The Hunt for Home,* G. Aiken
___HP646 *On Her Own,* W. E. Brunstetter

(If ordering from this page, please remember to include it with the order form.)

Presents

Great Inspirational Romance at a Great Price!

Heartsong Presents books are inspirational romances in contemporary and historical settings, designed to give you an enjoyable, spirit-lifting reading experience. You can choose wonderfully written titles from some of today's best authors like Wanda E. Brunstetter, Mary Connealy, Susan Page Davis, Cathy Marie Hake, Joyce Livingston, and many others.

When ordering quantities less than twelve, above titles are $2.97 each.
Not all titles may be available at time of order.

SEND TO: **Heartsong Presents** Readers' Service
P.O. Box 721, Uhrichsville, Ohio 44683

Please send me the items checked above. I am enclosing $ _____
(please add $3.00 to cover postage per order. OH add 7% tax. NJ add 6%). Send check or money order, no cash or C.O.D.s, please.
To place a credit card order, call 1-740-922-7280.

NAME _____

ADDRESS _____

CITY/STATE _____ ZIP_____

HP 11-07

HEARTSONG PRESENTS

If you love Christian romance…

$11.⁹⁹

You'll love Heartsong Presents' inspiring and faith-filled romances by today's very best Christian authors. . .Wanda E. Brunstetter, Mary Connealy, Susan Page Davis, Cathy Marie Hake, and Joyce Livingston, to mention a few!

When you join Heartsong Presents, you'll enjoy four brand-new, mass market, 176-page books—two contemporary and two historical—that will build you up in your faith when you discover God's role in every relationship you read about!

Mass Market 176 Pages

Imagine. . .four new romances every four weeks—with men and women like you who long to meet the one God has chosen as the love of their lives…all for the low price of $11.99 postpaid.

To join, simply visit www.heartsong presents.com or complete the coupon below and mail it to the address provided.

YES! Sign me up for Heartsong!

NEW MEMBERSHIPS WILL BE SHIPPED IMMEDIATELY!
Send no money now. We'll bill you only $11.99 postpaid with your first shipment of four books. Or for faster action, call 1-740-922-7280.

NAME _____

ADDRESS _____

CITY _____ STATE _____ ZIP _____

MAIL TO: HEARTSONG PRESENTS, P.O. Box 721, Uhrichsville, Ohio 44683
or sign up at **WWW.HEARTSONGPRESENTS.COM**